"Your mother'[...]" Rick said.

"I know." I looked down at the ground. "She saw my sketchbook."

"She told me."

"I don't think I like her discussing my problems with you."

"Why not? She's just trying to help you. You can't shut everybody out. You have to talk to someone."

"I don't think talking will help."

"I want to see those sketches that upset your mother and I want to look at that drawing of Nicky again."

"Maybe you should go home." I started up the steps toward the door.

Rick grabbed my arm. "What are you afraid of, Erin?"

"Nothing."

"The truth, Erin. Remember, we agreed to tell each other the truth."

"Maybe that's what I'm afraid of. The *truth*."

Books by Ann Gabhart

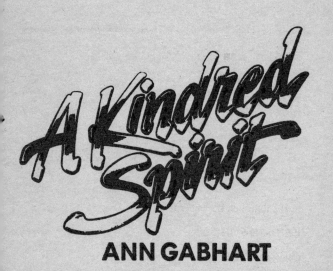

A Kindred Spirit

ANN GABHART

CROSSWINDS

New York • Toronto
Sydney • Auckland
Manila

First publication December 1987

ISBN 0-373-98013-2

Printed in the U.S.A.

RL 5.4, IL age 11 and up

ANN GABHART was born and brought up in Kentucky where she still lives. A real country girl, she is most happy when she is outdoors amid living and growing things. She began her very first book at the age of ten and has been writing ever since. Her three children have grown up to the sound of her typewriter clacking. Among her interests are reading, word games and basketball.

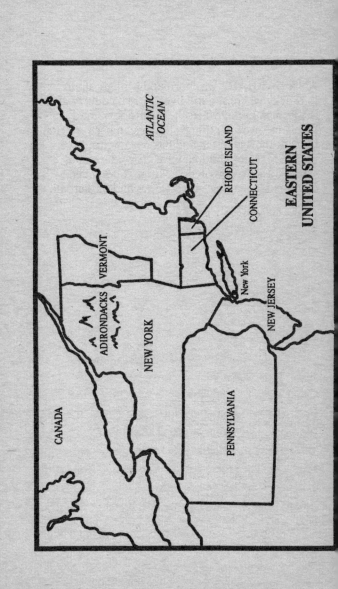

Chapter One

Rennie. Rennie.

I was so intent on my painting that I barely noticed the sound whispering through the tower room. Odd noises were always floating through the air up here anyway. The old rafters groaned, the wind played through the windows that circled the walls and birds scrambled in and out of their nests under the eaves. Then there were those noises nobody could explain although Mom liked to say it was Great-grandfather Winters rattling his chains.

Rennie.

This time the sound touched off an echo deep inside me, and my head came up. Dust motes clung to the bright sunshine flooding through the windows but nothing else.

Dabbing my paintbrush in first the blue, then the green, I turned all my attention back to the colors of a winter storm I was spreading on the canvas in front of me. The eyes surprised me. A stormy sky was no place for eyes. Yet they were there, and the only way they could have gotten there was through my brush. I stared at them while my heart began to beat heavily inside me.

"Erin," my mother called from the bottom of the steep stairs that led up to the tower room. "Erin?"

Even though I didn't answer, she climbed up to poke her head through the narrow door at the edge of the wall. "So here you are," she said. "I should have guessed."

"I was painting," I said softly.

"What's the matter? You look as if you'd seen a ghost. Not that that would be too surprising in this house."

"No ghost. It's just my painting."

"Is it that good?" The floorboards creaked as Mom crossed the room to stand beside me.

"It's these." I pointed toward the eyes. "I don't remember painting them into the picture."

"What are they?"

"Oh, Mother, they're eyes. Can't you see?"

"Eyes? Well, I guess they could sort of look like eyes if you used your imagination, but then no matter what you paint, I have to use my imagination to try to figure it out. I don't know why you can't just paint puppy dogs and kitty cats or rainbows like normal kids."

"I like painting colors and shapes."

"I know." Mom put her arm around me. "Don't get upset. I admire your creativity, but I'm too honest to claim I understand it." She studied the painting again. "Actually these sort of look like puppy-dog eyes except for the color. That blue—it's exactly the same as the color of your eyes, Erin."

"And yours." I looked at Mom.

"Yeah." She squeezed my shoulders. "Sometimes if it weren't for these eyes of ours I wouldn't be sure you were my daughter. I mean because you're an artist."

"I'm not an artist yet."

"I don't know how you can say that. Just look at all your paintings." She waved her hand at the canvases that leaned against the walls below the windows.

"They're not all good, and besides you just got through saying you never knew what any of them were."

"But I'm just an average mom and not an art critic."

"An average, slightly prejudiced mom." I kept my eyes away from the painting in front of me. "But you didn't climb up here to pump up my confidence. What did you want?"

"They're having a kind of reception, whatever, for me down at the library this afternoon. You know, a sort of meet-your-candidate kind of thing."

"And the family's supposed to be there so everybody can stare at us." I groaned.

"I know how you hate these things, Erin, but they're really important. Your father is going to come straight from the office and meet us there."

"I don't know why you couldn't have been happy being mayor. You could have won that job from now on without having to campaign at all."

"Maybe. Maybe not. And being mayor is nice, but..."

"But you want more. Just wait till I get away from home before you run for president."

"If I were running for president, it wouldn't matter if you were forty and living in the north of Alaska. They'd still find you to take your picture, but don't worry. State representative is a long way from the White House."

"Thank goodness." I put down my brush and slid my eyes quickly across the painting once more.

"You're a great kid," Mom said as she went back through the tower-room door. "Everybody who meets you is impressed that I could have such a wonderful daughter." Mom raised her voice an octave. "So pretty, so talented, so well-behaved and charming."

"I never know what to say."

"That's the reason they like you so much. You let them do all the talking, and when you smile at them, they're sure they've bridged the generation gap."

"Is this going to be all old ladies again?" I hesitated at the doorsill. I always hated to leave the tower room.

"The Concerned Citizens for a Better Tomorrow group have been very helpful to me," Mom said. "Without their support I'd have never been elected mayor to begin with, much less been able to run for representative."

"I know. They're sweet old ladies." With resignation I stepped through the door onto the first step.

Rennie.

I looked at Mom, but she had turned away from me and was going on down the stairs. "Did you hear that?" I asked.

Mom stopped and looked back at me. "What?"

"That noise."

Mom listened. "I can't hear anything. It was probably just the wind."

"It didn't sound like the wind."

"Then Great-grandfather Winters must be rattling his chains again."

"I suppose." As I looked back into the tower room, my eyes caught on the painting again.

"Come on, Erin. It wouldn't look good if I was late."

"Okay." With a jerk, I slammed the door shut, and the noise stopped. Maybe it had been the wind. Then again maybe the noise had never been anywhere but in my head.

The reception wasn't so bad. I counted fifteen people there who didn't have gray hair. Two or three people were even almost my age if you counted Mrs. Harris's thirteen-year-old grandson. Mrs. Harris was the president of the Concerned Citizens group and where Mrs. Harris went, Jason went. It was more fun talking to the old ladies.

I didn't have to talk much to anyone that day. I'd found a good spot—visible yet out of the main flow of people. I could stand there nodding and smiling and appearing to be right in the middle of a dozen conversations without ever saying a word to anyone. It helped that I had a cup of punch in my hand. My hands always gave me away when I felt ill at ease at these "functions," as Mom called them.

Mom thrived on them. She was a born politician who not only enjoyed everything about campaigning, but also felt a deep responsibility and commitment to those she was elected to serve. While I'd been joking in the tower room about her running for president, I didn't doubt at all that she might get to the governor's mansion in time.

I watched her work the group as she listened to each person with genuine interest and called everybody by name. I'd seen her go into a group of strangers, and by the time she'd worked through them, she knew not only their names and voting status but the names and ages of their children and grandchildren as well.

She loved the crowds while I would have given anything to be away from them all and back in my tower room with a paintbrush in my hand. What was I going to do about those eyes in my painting?

Mrs. Harris interrupted my thoughts. "Erin, dear, I've got somebody for you to talk to."

I started to tell her I didn't care whether I talked to Jason or not, but I bit back the words. If I had to listen to him describe his latest computer program in detail, then I would just have to listen.

Holding back a sigh, I turned to face her, but it wasn't Jason she had in tow.

"This is Richard Lucas," she said. "He and his parents moved down here from Ohio just last year."

"Rick. Not Richard. Rick Lucas." The boy kept his eyes on me.

"Oh yes, of course," Mrs. Harris said. "And Richard, this is Erin, our candidate's charming daughter." She beamed at us, patting first my arm and then his before she rushed away.

Suddenly the punch cup in my hand felt awkward, and I turned to put it on the table behind me before I dropped it. I knew Rick Lucas. All the girls at Brookfield High did. Not only was he great looking; he had this special air about him as well. At school he kept to himself most of the time, and his quiet aloofness intrigued the girls. Still, no matter what they tried, none of the girls I knew had gotten him to say much more than hi.

There was a smile in his brown eyes when I turned back to him. "So I'm finally going to get to meet the candidate's perfectly wonderful daughter, or is it wonderfully perfect?"

My own smile faded. "I'm not sure either of those adjectives fit."

"Oh, yes, perfect is the perfect word. Always smiling, always doing what you're supposed to be doing, never in trouble, never mad. Definitely perfect."

I forced my sweetest smile as I said, "It's been perfectly wonderful talking to you, Richard, but I believe I'll go find Jason. I haven't had a chance to talk to him all afternoon."

He laughed. "See, I told you. Perfect. Especially the 'Richard.'" As I began turning away, he put his hand on my arm to stop me. "You don't really want to talk to Jason. I've talked to him already, and though he's surely a genius, the details of his latest feat aren't too interesting."

"I like computers," I lied.

"I do, too, just not talking about them." His hand was still on my arm. "Look, stay here, and I promise not to insult you any more by saying how wonderful you are."

I couldn't quite keep from laughing. "What are you doing at this kind of function anyway? You don't look like the average Concerned Citizen member."

"I registered to vote two weeks ago. How better to cast a knowledgeable vote in my first election than by meeting the candidate face to face?"

"Am I supposed to be impressed?"

"Of course. Actually most of it is true. But I also have to do a project for this political science class I'm taking, and I thought following an actual campaign would be ideal."

"So you picked my mother."

"She's the only one in the neighborhood, and it looks like she's done a fairly good job as mayor. These people seem to like her," he said as he looked over the crowd.

"I'm sure she'd appreciate your consideration when you vote."

He looked back at me. "Do you ever say anything that isn't rehearsed?" He added quickly, "Oh, sorry, I promised not to insult you anymore, but do you?"

"Not at this kind of thing if I can help it. I'm just here as a kind of decoration. My mother's the one who has to do the real talking."

"Sounds boring for you."

"But necessary."

"What would you be doing right now if you had your choice?"

"That's easy. Painting." I glanced out the large front windows. The sunlight, though still bright, was softer now as the day edged toward evening. "The light's just about perfect at this time of day."

"What do you paint?" Rick moved a little closer.

"All kinds of things or the illusion of their shapes and colors anyway."

"You're an artist?"

"I'd like to be," I said, noticing his surprised look. "Why? Don't I fit your image of an aspiring artist?"

"I don't think I've ever met an aspiring artist, but I would have imagined one to be a shade more exotic, flamboyant, or something."

"My paintings turn out a little exotic sometimes. At least Mom thinks so."

"Now you've got me curious. I'll have to come see for myself."

"But you haven't been invited," I said. "I don't let just anybody see my work."

"But you'll show your paintings to me, won't you?"

I thought about taking him up to the tower room to look at my paintings, and my heart speeded up even as I said, "No, I don't think so."

His heavy, dark eyebrows pulled together in a puzzled frown. "Why not?"

"I don't know you well enough." What I didn't say was that I didn't need a critic, and I could easily imagine Rick Lucas making fun of my work.

"Don't know me well enough? Well, we can fix that. Come on. Let's get some more punch, and I'll tell you my life story."

"I don't think we'll have time. It looks like they're closing the punch bowl down."

"So they are," he said. "And here comes my mother ready to leave."

"Mother? I thought you were here because you were a concerned voter who wanted to make an intelligent choice."

He grinned but didn't say anything as a trim, middle-aged woman came up to us. "Leave it to Rick to corner the prettiest girl in the room," she said.

"Mom, this is Erin, Mayor Winters's daughter."

"Yes, of course I already knew that," Mrs. Lucas said, her eyes on me. "I've heard so much about your whole family, since we arrived in Brookdale. Being a history buff, I've especially enjoyed the stories about your grandfather, Judge Winters."

"Great-grandfather," I corrected. "I don't remember him. He died shortly after I was born."

"What a shame you never got to know him although I'm sure you feel almost as though you had from all the stories you've heard. Now here's your mother with every chance of becoming the next state representative. Did Rick tell you he's interested in politics?"

"He said something about it," I said.

"We're both planning to volunteer to help with your mother's campaign. You know, at the grass-roots level. So I'm sure we'll be seeing a lot of you, too."

"I'll look forward to it, Mrs. Lucas," I said with a smile.

"Perfect," Rick whispered as he eased close to me. "You must practice in front of a mirror."

I wouldn't watch him leave even if I did want to. Instead I deliberately moved across the room to where Jason was shoving the last of the cookies in his mouth. "Hi, Jason," I said. "What have you been up to?"

As Jason began talking, I let my eyes slide over to the door where Rick's mother was saying her good-byes to my mother and Mrs. Harris. Rick was watching me. "Perfect." He mouthed the word and then smiled.

Chapter Two

On the way home from the reception, the word *perfect* kept running through my head like a taunt, and I began to hope I'd never see Rick Lucas again. I didn't care if he was the best-looking guy in the senior class at Brookdale. If he was at any more of Mom's political gatherings, I'd still give him a wide berth and latch on to Jason early. Just the thought made me yawn. My ears were still ringing with "bits and bytes."

Deliberately I turned my mind away from both Rick Lucas and Jason's latest genius project to my half-finished painting at home. It would be too dark to work on it now. While the tower room made a wonderful studio in the daylight hours, at night the shadows took over, and even with the lights Dad had installed, it was hard to get a true perspective on depth and colors.

Mom interrupted my thoughts. "Thanks, Erin. You were perfect as usual today."

"Perfect? I didn't do anything but stand there and smile and say, 'Yes, school is fine.' I don't see how you can say that's perfect unless you mean perfectly dull."

"Was it that bad?" Mom glanced over at me. "And I thought you were probably having more fun than usual with that Rick Lucas there. He is cuter than the average Concerned Citizen member, you'll have to admit."

"It wasn't that bad. I just don't think I'm perfect."

Mom put her hand over mine on the seat. "You're a perfect daughter for me."

"If anybody's perfect, it's you. The perfect candidate."

Mom put her hand back on the steering wheel and clutched it so tightly that her knuckles turned white. "I hope so. I really want to win."

"You will. You always win any election you're in."

"That's in Brookdale where the Winters's name pulls a lot of weight. It'll be different out in the district. I'll have to campaign on more than my name, rather your father's name, and I'm going to need a lot of help."

"The Concerned Citizens and I will do whatever we can."

"I'm counting on it." Mom watched the road for a minute before she went on. "What did you think of the Lucas boy? Did you already know him?"

"I knew who he was."

"He says he wants to help with the campaign."

"Yeah, he told me. Some kind of project for one of his classes."

"But his mother told me he was really interested in politics."

"Then you're going to let him help?"

"I don't see why not. He's a registered voter, and just because he's young doesn't mean he shouldn't take part in the political process. Besides, anybody can address envelopes and hand out flyers at meetings." Mom grinned over at me as she pulled into our driveway. "And it should make the campaign much more interesting for you. A cute guy like that hanging around."

"He's cute. Too cute for me."

"How can you say that? You're probably the prettiest girl in school. Maybe I should quit campaigning for political office and start entering you in beauty contests. You'd be the next Miss America."

"Oh, Mom, you know I'm not going to enter any beauty contests."

"I know, honey. I was just kidding." Mom pushed open the car door before she looked around and said, "But you would win. There's no doubt about that. I wish I could be as sure I'd win."

Later, as I got ready for bed, I rinsed the soap off my face and stared at myself in the mirror. I wasn't at all sure I was pretty as Mom had said. My skin was clear and pale. Even in the middle of the summer, I couldn't get more than a touch of a tan. My hair was almost black and wavy but really wouldn't curl. Of course, I had to admit that my eyes were unusual enough to be almost pretty. I stared at the reflection of my eyes until they almost seemed to belong to someone else.

I'd never even seen a model in a magazine with the same color blue eyes I had, only my mother. And it was a blue without a name. It wasn't sky blue, aqua blue, teal blue, any blue color I'd seen in all my searches through color catalogues. Before today, I'd never been able to mix that exact color of blue. Now without even knowing how I'd done it, the blue was in my painting up in the tower room.

The air dried the water on my face as I went up the steps that led to the tower room. Mom and Dad had gone to another meeting, and I was home alone.

Climbing the stairs slowly, I kept wondering if the eyes would still be there. Perhaps I'd imagined it all. Maybe now when I looked there would be only the heavy grays and purplish blacks of a stormy sky with the streaks of lighter colors running through them.

I didn't turn on any lights as I made my way through the house to the tower room. I'd never been afraid of the dark in spite of all Mom's talk about Great-grandfather Winters's ghost.

I wasn't exactly afraid now even though a strange chill whispered down along my spine. As I climbed up to the tower, I remembered the day long ago when I'd discovered the door ajar and ventured up the steep steps into a wonderland of light.

From the very first moment I had sat in the middle of the room with sunshine streaming in through the windows to wrap warm fingers of light around me, the tower room had been my special place. With my crayons and paper spread out around me, I'd spent hours on the dusty floor, drawing the rainbows and butterflies Mom wished I was drawing now.

At first my mother had tried everything to keep me from climbing the steps to the room, but nothing had worked. Finally she'd given up and made plans to transform the room into a playroom. When I saw the man she'd hired measuring and banging on the walls, I pitched the only real fit I'd ever had. I was soundly punished, which I deserved, but more important, the man with his tools had been sent away. The tower room remained untouched.

I didn't know why. I only knew I needed the wood floors to stay bare and the windows to remain uncurtained. I thought then it might be because of Nicky. Only later did I realize that I had a need for plain surroundings when I was painting.

The dozens of lights were the only modern feature in the room, but now I didn't touch the panel on the wall that controlled them. Enough moonlight came through the windows so that I could see that the eyes were still very much a part of the painting. I backed away from the easel and dropped down on the window seat.

Most of the time when I went to the tower room at night, I watched the lights of the town shift on and off around us. I'd lean back hardly thinking while images of new shapes and colors would drift through my mind, but tonight my eyes were drawn again and again to the painting in the middle of the room.

My paintings had surprised me before when something I'd been working on suddenly showed up different from what I expected. But the eyes had not merely formed out of a shape that I was working on. They had appeared out of nowhere and seemed almost alive. Even before the echo of the name began floating through the air once more, the eyes were awakening a response deep inside me that I'd thought was gone forever.

Rennie. Rennie.

The name circled the room, bouncing off the windows and ceiling. It was my name, a call from the past.

Sitting very still, I shut my eyes and concentrated on emptying my mind. The sound whirled faster in the room as though in anguish.

Rennie. Rennie!

When I felt as though I might explode if I didn't answer, I said, "I'm here."

The name whispered once more through the room. I knew he had come even before I opened my eyes.

He wavered there in front of the painting, just a shadow, and even as I watched, he faded a bit. It wasn't the Nicky I remembered, but it was Nicky. An older Nicky, a sadder Nicky.

"Don't go away," I said softly, repeating the words I'd always used as a child whenever Nicky appeared to me. "Stay and play."

His image came back a little stronger, and he glided closer to my window seat. Though his mouth moved, I heard no sound. I reached toward him, but I didn't touch him. We'd never touched even as children. At the same time he reached toward me, and once more the sound whispered through the room. *Rennie.*

"Are you really here, Nicky?" And then I thought that was a foolish question. I wasn't sure Nicky had ever really been there.

Again, although he seemed to answer, no sound came forth, and silence settled around us. He was still blond just as I remembered him, but he was no longer the little boy who had come to play with me years ago. He had grown and changed. His eyes were the same, though, the same blue as my own. I could see that plainly even though his other features were blurred. His eyes were vivid, just like the ones in the painting.

I wondered how different I looked to him. It had been so long since we had been together.

A thousand memories rushed back. Until I was ten, Nicky had come often to visit. The name Rennie would whisper in my mind, and then he'd be there beside me laughing and ready to play. At first it hadn't mattered where we were. Mom hadn't minded me talking to a playmate she couldn't see. Lots of only children invented playmates, she had assured me more than once. But then when Nicky kept coming to visit even after I had begun school and made real-life friends, she had started taking me to the doctors. That was when Nicky and I began to use the tower room for his visits.

"Why did you come back?" I whispered. "I thought you'd gone forever."

His eyes filled with tears.

"Nicky, what's wrong?" I asked as he began fading away. "Don't go. Tell me what's wrong."

He slowly closed his eyes, and as soon as he did the rest of his body disappeared. I reached out to feel the air where he'd been standing.

"Nicky!" I cried. But the moonlight stayed empty, and my cry went unanswered.

I don't know how much time passed before Mom pushed open the door and said, "Erin, are you up here?"

I tried twice before I managed to answer.

She came into the room. "What are you doing sitting up here in the dark?"

"The moon's shining."

When she hit the panel on the wall, I shielded my eyes from the light that flooded the room.

"It's late," Mom said.

I kept my hand shading my eyes. "I lost track of the time."

"You should bring a clock up here." She came closer and looked at me. "Is something wrong, Erin? Are you sick?"

I dropped my hand away from my eyes.

Mom frowned. "You look as if you'd seen a ghost."

"Nicky. Nicky came back."

"What are you talking about, Erin?"

"You know what I'm talking about, Mama. Nicky, but he was different. He didn't smile."

Mom's eyes never left my face. "You must have fallen asleep. It was just a dream."

"No, Mom. He was here." I jumped off my seat. "Why can't you believe he was here?"

"Oh, Erin, not again. Not now." She turned away from me and back to the door. When I didn't follow her, she cleared her throat and said, "Aren't you coming, dear? It's really time you should be in bed. Tomorrow's a school day, you know."

I stood still. "I did see him. He was here."

"I just can't deal with it tonight, Erin," she said without looking at me. "We'll talk about it tomorrow. Now come along to bed."

I took a deep breath. "Okay. I'll be down in a minute."

She looked at me again. "It was a dream, Erin. A dream."

"A dream," I whispered to myself as I slowly followed her down the steps.

Chapter Three

When I got home from school the next day, I stayed away from the tower room. I didn't want to think about the eyes or Nicky.

Mom, too, pretended that nothing had happened—at least not until after we'd eaten supper. She had another meeting, but she didn't hurry as we cleared off the table.

"I'll wash up," I offered. "You'll be late."

"Those meetings never start on time," she said as she slowly piled up the plates. Then she sat them on the sink with a clatter and turned to me. "I called Dr. Carruthers today."

My hand seemed to be moving in slow motion as I wiped the crumbs off the table.

"She says maybe you should come in for a talk," Mom said.

"I don't want to talk to Dr. Carruthers." The chicken we'd had for supper gathered in a hard knot inside me.

I didn't look at Mom as I went to the sink and started filling the dishpan. Instead I concentrated on the soap bubbles forming on top of the water and tried not to remember all the hours I'd spent with Dr. Carruthers. Wasted hours. Hours she had used trying to convince me that Nicky wasn't real. The bubbles foamed up and over the lip of the pan, and I pushed the faucets off.

Gathering up a handful of bubbles, I held them up to let the light play colors through them, but I couldn't get lost in the colors of the prism now. Mom was waiting for me to say something.

"I've been thinking, Mom," I said and blew the bubbles back into the dishpan. "It could be that it was a dream after all. I was tired. I might have dozed off."

"Of course it was a dream, Erin. Still Dr. Carruthers thinks it would be a good idea if you came in for a visit."

"Why? Does she want to write a book about troubled adolescents?"

"You're being unfair, Erin. Dr. Carruthers never mentioned your name in the book she wrote."

"No. How did it go?" I changed my voice as I went on. "'A child I'll call Susan to protect the identity of the patient, a lonely child with no siblings, uses her highly developed imagination to draw forth a playmate, a brother. Poor Susan, she's a little nutso, but not too bad. With the proper treatment, she might even be able to live a normal life.'"

"That's enough, Erin," Mom said sharply.

"Why? That's what she wrote, wasn't it?"

"You were a case study."

"I didn't want to be a case study, and I won't be a case study now."

"Another doctor, then. Dr. Carruthers knows you feel some resentment toward her, and she said she'd be glad to recommend someone else. But she thinks it's important that you talk to somebody."

"I'm talking to somebody. I'm talking to you right now."

Mom went on as though I hadn't spoken. "She says this campaign could be bringing it back for you. That maybe I'm too busy, gone too much. She thinks maybe you're afraid that if I win, I won't have time for you anymore."

"Don't be silly, Mom. I'm old enough to take care of myself now, and I want you to win."

"Dr. Carruthers says we sometimes can't know what we want. That even when we think we feel one way our subconscious is feeling another."

"I know. I've heard it all before. Nicky was just a product of my subconscious, a playmate I conjured up whenever I felt lonely. Harmless enough as long as I didn't let it get out of hand and start thinking he was real or something." I began washing the glasses slowly, watching intently for a catch of color. "Well, you don't have to worry, Mom. We've already decided it was only a dream."

"But Dr. Carruthers says dreams are often windows to our subconscious."

I concentrated on the rinse water sliding off the glass and didn't say anything.

After a long time, Mom went on. "I want to make you an appointment. If not with Dr. Carruthers, then someone else."

"No, Mom. No doctors." I sat the glass in the drainer. "It was a dream. Everybody has dreams. Even you."

Mom was quiet a minute before she said, "I've got to go. I'm going to be late."

After Mom left, the clink of the dishes in the sink was extra loud. Usually I liked the way the silence of the house settled around me when I was alone. It gave me time to think, but tonight I was almost afraid to think.

I looked up at a spot just beyond the light and willed my mind to go blank. Sometimes I could pull black velvet over my thoughts, smothering them until colors and shapes began seeping through and the idea for a new painting surfaced naturally.

Tonight the thoughts were too frantic to be smothered out. I couldn't keep from thinking about all the doctors who had combed through my childhood. They had searched for reasons for Nicky in the way I loved my mother, in the way my mother loved me, in the way I responded to word tests, even in the way I drew. They would give me paper and crayons and ask me to draw pictures for them to interpret.

I hated it, all of it. But after a while I made a game of it, taking turns drawing pictures I thought they would approve of with pictures so outrageous that now when I remember them, I wonder why they didn't advise Mom to have me committed. Then again, maybe they had.

Dumping the dishwater, I listened to it gurgle down the drain. I wouldn't go back to the doctors. No matter what. Perhaps Nicky had been a dream just as I'd told Mom. It was possible, maybe even probable.

As I found my algebra book to start on my homework, I thought it would be better if it were a dream. Much better.

I didn't go back to the tower room for three days. I wanted to, though. I even started up the steps several times, but something always stopped me. Although I knew I was afraid to go up, I wasn't sure which frightened me the most—that Nicky would come or that he wouldn't.

Still I couldn't stay away from the tower room forever. I needed to paint. Of course I had my sketchbook downstairs, and I had been filling up pages with rough sketches of anything and everything. But that wasn't the same as painting.

I'd even made a few sketches of Rick Lucas. Since Sunday I'd been noticing him more often at school, but no matter how much I studied him, I couldn't get his face to turn out right in my sketches. I began to worry that my hand was out and that nothing I drew or painted was going to be right.

Thursday when I got home from school, I planned to throw down my books and hit the tower-room steps in a run. I wouldn't give myself time to think about it.

I was halfway there when Mom stopped me. "Erin, is that you?"

Reluctantly I retraced my steps and found her at the dining-room table along with Mrs. Harris and Mrs. Lucas.

"Mom. I didn't know you were home," I said with a nod and a smile to the other women.

"We've got about a million and three envelopes to address," Mom said. "Maybe if you don't have too much homework you can help us for a while."

"Sure," I answered quickly. "Just as soon as I run upstairs and change."

I was turning for the stairs again when Mrs. Lucas said, "I thought Rick was going to come over with you from school."

"Was he?" I looked back at her. "I didn't know."

"Didn't he talk to you today?"

"He didn't say anything about coming over."

"That Rick." Mrs. Lucas shook her head. "He's a mystery sometimes, but I guess he'll come on over in a few minutes."

"I guess so," I said and made my escape.

What I didn't tell Mrs. Lucas was that I had talked to Rick that day. He'd stopped me in the hall with a "How's Miss Perfect today?"

Smiling sweetly, I'd managed to let myself be swept away from him by a group of kids passing by.

He'd called after me, "Wait up, Erin."

I'd pretended not to hear. All through the next class I'd wondered why Rick had wanted to talk to me and had imagined all sorts of things until I'd wished I could go back out in the hall and play the scene over again. I'd looked for him the rest of the day, but our paths hadn't crossed again.

Now I knew he just wanted to know about working on Mom's campaign. It had nothing really to do with me at all. I yanked off my school clothes and threw them on my bed.

I picked out one of my better sweaters and was about to pull it on when I realized what I was doing. There was no need in me getting dressed up because Rick Lucas might show up at the house. I slipped on my oldest pair of warm-ups instead.

Rick wasn't interested in me as a girl, only as the candidate's daughter, and tonight there weren't going to be any camera flashes popping. I could look like a slob if I wanted to. And suddenly I wanted to.

As I passed the tower-room steps on the way back down, I hesitated a minute, wanting to go up. Yet at the same time I felt almost relieved to have an excuse to stay away. But how much longer could I go without making a brush stroke on canvas? Sketching satisfied the itching in my hand, but the yearning in my soul needed more. Even when I was painting, that yearning feeling never quite went away. In my mind, there was always something beyond that I needed to see and capture.

Now on top of all that was Nicky. Quickly, before I could think anymore about it, I ran downstairs and into the dining room.

Rick had come while I was upstairs, and in spite of myself I wished I could run back and put on something a little nicer than my red sweats.

"Hi, Erin," he said. "I'm sorry we didn't get a chance to talk today."

"Yeah, well, I see you found the house okay on your own."

"Of course. Everybody in Brookdale knows where the ancestral home of the Winters's family is. You're a landmark."

With a frown, Mrs. Lucas looked up from her stack of envelopes and said, "Ricky."

Mrs. Harris butted in. "Richard's absolutely right, Helen. I keep trying to get Janet to put the house on the historical registry."

"Now, Evelyn," Mom said. "I just haven't had time. And besides, though it might look like a chunk of history to you, it's just home to us."

"For how many generations?" Rick asked while his mother's frown deepened.

"Four anyway," Mom said. "I don't know the history of the family as well as I should, but Thomas could tell you. Are you interested in genealogy?"

"You could say that," Rick said.

"Genealogy and politics. Sort of a weird mixture, don't you think?" I said.

"Erin, don't be rude," Mom said.

"Erin rude? She wouldn't know how," Rick said with a laugh. "Actually the two mix better than you think sometimes."

"Ricky," his mother said quietly. "We came over to help Mrs. Winters stuff envelopes, not lobby for any kind of political action."

Mom laughed, taking away the odd tension that had settled over the table. "It might be a little early to lobby any issue with me. I haven't won yet."

"Oh, but you will, Janet," Mrs. Harris said. "Don't worry. You will."

"Yeah, Mom, think positive. You'll win because you're the best candidate." I picked up one of the flyers we were mailing out. "If you don't believe it, just read one of these. Now do you want me to fold, stuff or address?"

"I'll fold and stuff, and you can address," Rick said. "My handwriting's not so great, but I'm sure yours is perfect."

I took the list Mom handed me and sat down beside Rick. Determined not to let him bother me, I tackled the list of names. I knew about mailings. I'd been helping Mom with them since she first ran for the school board when I was six.

Rick and I worked without talking while the voices of the three women floated gently around us as they discussed the weather, which was fine for this time of the year, the kinds of flowers they wanted to plant when they got the time, and the people who'd been at the last meeting of the Concerned Citizens group. Mrs. Harris mentioned how well Jason was doing in school at least three times.

After a while, Mom and Mrs. Harris had to leave for a meeting with some kind of committee. Mrs. Lucas, Rick and I worked on for a half hour before Mrs. Lucas said, "I guess we'd better go too, Rick."

"Erin's not finished," Rick said.

The folded, stuffed envelopes were piled high beside me. "That's okay. I can work on these later, but I know Mom really appreciates your help. Nobody ever wins an election by herself."

Mrs. Lucas smiled, and Rick grinned as he said, "Go on, Mom. I'll just stay a little longer and help Erin with a few of these."

"I thought you said nobody could read your handwriting," I said.

"So I'll print."

Mrs. Lucas hesitated, once again frowning. "Don't look so worried, Mom," Rick said. "I promise to be nice."

After Mrs. Lucas left, the silence settled over us as we worked. The only sound was the scratch of our pens on the envelopes.

After writing ten addresses, Rick looked over his shoulder. "Gad, you can feel your ancestors breathing down your necks around here. Is this place haunted?"

I smiled a little. "I don't think so although every once in a while we do hear some strange noises."

Rick threw down his pen and stared at me. "It might be fun to be haunted by your ancestors."

"I doubt it."

"I don't," he said firmly. "I'd like it."

"Are you always so sure about everything?" I began a new address.

"Of course," Rick said, watching me. "Except about who I am."

"What do you mean who you are? Everybody knows who they are. Are you having a self-identity crisis or amnesia?" I didn't look up at him but kept writing.

"Amnesia, I guess you could say. Amnesia of the past."

"I don't know what you're talking about."

"You don't know what you're writing, either." Rick pointed at my envelope and then the list. "The name was Nathaniel, not Nicky."

I stared at the address I'd written. Then with fingers that trembled I tore open the flap and took out the flyer before crumpling the envelope.

Rick was still talking. "The reason you don't know what I'm talking about is that things are too perfect for you. Here you are in this house surrounded by your past. Your roots must go down miles and miles, and you'll never have to wonder where you came from, what makes you the way you are. You'll know. Perhaps it was Great-grandmother Elizabeth who had eyes like yours or Great-great-grandfather Perry. Whatever, you can look back and know exactly what your family was like, but I can't. I've been dropped out of nowhere into blank space with nothing behind me."

I threw the envelope away, but I didn't take up my pen again. I was afraid to, and as I sat there listening to Rick, trying hard to make sense of his words, a shiver ran through me. "Everybody comes from somewhere," I said softly, thinking of Nicky.

"Oh, I know that. I came from somewhere too. I just don't know where. You see, I'm adopted."

"That's why you're nothing like your mother." I apologized at once. "I shouldn't have said that."

"Don't take it back. I like you better when you aren't making practiced, perfect answers."

I stood up. "I think it's time you went home." I began sorting the envelopes into different, meaningless piles.

"Why? Things are just now getting interesting."

"You came to help Mom address envelopes. We're not going to address any more envelopes this afternoon."

"I want to see your paintings."

"No," I said.

"Why not? I've told you my dark secret, that I'm adopted, probably an illegitimate child and definitely unwanted."

"Your parents now want you."

"But I want to know about my birth parents, and I'm going to find out about them, too. Somehow. Some way," Rick said. "Now I want to go look at your paintings."

"Not today."

"I won't take no for an answer."

"You'll have to." I started toward the front door. "Thanks again for helping us with the mailing."

He followed me and went through the door. Stopping on the porch, he turned back and said, "I'm going to see your paintings sooner or later, Erin."

"Maybe later." Then before he could say another word, I shut the door in his face and ran for the tower room.

Chapter Four

*R*ennie.

I heard it as soon as I pushed back the door, but the sound was faint, disappearing.

Afraid again, I hesitated in the doorway. I couldn't pretend to be dreaming this time. Maybe it would be better if I shut the door on the sound and went back downstairs, but I couldn't. I went slowly on through the door into the tower room.

"Nicky," I whispered. "Don't go away. Stay and play." The only answer was a faint stir in the air. Nothing else. With tears pushing at my eyes, I remembered other times when I had raced to the tower room too late.

I straightened my mouth firmly and told myself I was glad. According to the doctors, Nicky had never been anything more than a figment of my imagination anyway.

"Erin, can I come in?"

"Nicky." I whirled around so quickly that I knocked over the easel. When I saw Rick standing there, I was too surprised to speak.

"Sorry. I didn't mean to startle you." Rick looked around as he came into the tower room. "Is someone else up here with you?"

"You had no right to follow me up here." I glared at him as anger flooded through me.

"I know, and I'm sorry. But I thought maybe there was something wrong."

"Something wrong? What do you mean?"

"I mean Miss Perfect shoves me out the door and then slams it in my face."

"Don't call me that."

"Anyway, I didn't want you to be too mad at me. A little mad maybe, but not too mad, so I came back in to apologize for whatever had upset you and you were flying up the stairs. I guess I shouldn't have, but I followed you. Like I said before, I'm sorry if I scared you."

I sank down on the floor beside my half-finished painting. The fall didn't seem to have hurt it, and I gently ran my hand over the ridges of paint. I was afraid I was going to burst into tears at any second. "Go away, Rick. Please."

He came over and looked down at me. "Erin, who's Nicky?"

I stared at him a moment before I said, "I don't know." I looked away from him back to the painting. Nicky's eyes watched me out of the dark tones of the storm clouds.

"Do you want to tell me about him?" Rick squatted down beside me.

I kept my eyes on the painting. "I don't think I could even if I wanted to. It's all so strange."

"I promise not to laugh." Reaching out, he covered my hand with his.

"I don't know how you can promise that." I pulled my hand away. "You've been making fun of me ever since we were introduced."

"Only because I like you." He took my hand again.

Our eyes caught and held. Finally I said, "Do you still want to see my paintings?"

"Let me help you set this one back up first."

We righted the easel and carefully placed the canvas back on it. Rick stood studying it while my heartbeat began racing. Since the light was fading outside, I turned on the overhead lights. My hand trembled. I'd never shown my work to an outsider before.

As the minutes ticked by, I stared at the canvas with him, trying to see it through his eyes. I had been trying to capture the feel of winter clouds threatening on the horizon but never coming closer.

"It's different," he said finally.

I laughed a little. "That's what people say when they don't like something, but they don't want to hurt the other person's feelings."

"Okay. Maybe I should say it's oppressive."

"Good. That's sort of what I'm trying to get out of the colors, but it's not right yet. I may never get it right."

"Why the eyes?"

"The eyes don't belong. I didn't aim to put them there, but there they are."

"Can't you paint over them?"

"I'm not sure. I haven't tried yet."

"Haven't you got anything cheerier to look at?"

"I've got *Sun Drops*." Bright yellow splatters in different sizes covered the canvas I pointed out. "It's the first thing I did in oils."

When he didn't say anything, I rushed on. "I know it's not too good, but I had a lot of fun with it. Nothing I've done is great, but I'm learning. Someday I'll be able to get the colors I feel down on the canvas in the right way."

He walked slowly around the walls, stopping to look at first one canvas then another. "These are all yours?"

I nodded shyly. "Mom says I'm obsessed." Watching him, I began to feel stretched and brittle till one wrong word might snap me in two.

"I'm surprised," he said when his tour of the walls was over.

"Why?"

"I expected trees and houses, butterflies and rainbows, maybe animals, but nothing like this."

I looked at the paintings. "That's what they are. The colors of those things set free as best I can. Which isn't too good yet."

"I won't pretend to understand them or even like them, but I am impressed." Rick looked at me. "I think I want to know more about the artist who painted them."

"There's not a lot to know."

"I don't believe that," Rick said. "Just the way I won't believe that I shouldn't know more about myself and the kind of people I came from."

"But what if you find out something you'd rather not know?"

"About you or about myself?"

"Either." I looked away from him.

"It's better to know than to wonder," Rick said quietly. "Believe me. I've done a lot of wondering."

We were at the bottom of the stairs when Mom came in. She looked at us and then toward the dining room where she could just glimpse the table with its stack of envelopes. "Still working?" she asked.

"Rick wanted to see my paintings," I said.

Mom's eyes came back to us, sharper this time, but though questions raced across her face, she only said, "That's nice." She turned to Rick. "I'm not sure where Erin gets her artistic talent. Certainly not from me. I can't even understand what she's doing half the time."

"Neither can I," I said, and we all laughed before Rick said his goodbyes quickly and left.

After he was gone, Mom looked at me again, and I was glad for the dim light in the hallway. "Are you okay, Erin?"

"Sure, Mom. How'd the meeting go?"

"All right. I think we might get funding for the new sidewalk, and everybody's excited about the planning for the park. I think they're going to name it after your Great-grandfather Winters. That'll make him rattle his chains for sure."

"Was Dad pleased?"

"Of course he was. He'll be along in a few minutes." Mom slipped off her jacket and hung it up. "Come on, and we can talk while you help me get dinner on the table before he gets here. Then the two of you will have to help me finish up the mailing."

I groaned, but I didn't really mind. Working on the mailings with Mom and Dad had always been fun, a time to talk and share and laugh over the odd names we came across on the lists. Tonight was no different.

Once when we heard the boards creak over our heads, Dad looked up and said, "Grandfather Winters must have heard about the park, and he's up there practicing his ribbon-cutting speech."

"You don't really believe in ghosts, do you, Dad?"

"Absolutely not," Dad said and then added with a grin, "Except, of course, Grandfather Winters. He couldn't go on to heaven and trust us with the running of Brookdale. That wouldn't do at all."

"Oh, Dad, you're being silly," I said, glad that he was. Nicky didn't come nudging into my mind more than twice as I copied all the names correctly without a hitch.

The next day at school I was nervous about seeing Rick again. I was sure I wouldn't know what to say, that though I had been comfortable with him in the tower room, it would be different in the school corridors. I managed to avoid running into him all morning.

At lunch, he took matters into his own hands and simply brought his tray over and sat down beside me. It was that easy.

The next few days were busy. I helped Mom with her campaigning, and we all went to the ground-breaking for the Granville A. Winters Community Park. Dad made Great-grandfather Winters's speech for him—all about the good feeling public servants got from serving their community in the best way

possible. After the crowd started applauding, I knew
that it was only a matter of time until Dad would be
running for some kind of office, too. And I wondered how I could have been born into a family of
politicians.

Every chance I got, I tried to work on my painting, but after hours passed with only a few meaningless brush strokes, I removed the canvas from the
easel and placed it facedown against the wall.

I'd never given up on a painting before, even when
it didn't seem right. But I couldn't paint the eyes out,
and I couldn't continue with the eyes there.

They were Nicky's eyes. Yet I felt no whisper of his
presence as the days passed. Once or twice before I
turned the painting to the wall, I called to him, begging him to appear. The wind whistled through the
windows, but there was no echo of Rennie to the
lonesome sound.

Still, every day I climbed up to the tower room and
tried to work with colors that were suddenly stubborn and flat while I waited.

When I came down from the tower room, Rick
was usually waiting for me. He didn't track me down
by coming up to the tower room again, and I was
glad. Nicky would never come if there was a stranger
around.

Rick wasn't there just to see me anyway. He was in
and out of the house and had become as much a part
of the campaign as Mrs. Harris. His class project was

going well, and though Mom's winning or losing had
no bearing on his grade, Rick began to get caught up
in the excitement of the campaign. He grabbed kids
in the halls at school and insisted they should regis-
ter to vote if they were old enough.

Together we went to neighboring towns, stood on
street corners and handed out cards and flyers. I
hated it, but Rick loved it.

As the days raced by toward the election, Rick and
I worked harder than ever, but we still found time to
talk. Mostly about him.

I found out that he'd been adopted by the Lu-
cases when he was three days old and told as soon as
he could understand the words that he'd been cho-
sen by them. It wasn't until this past year that Rick
had begun to wonder about his biological parents.

"I don't want another mother. Mom understands
that, thank goodness," Rick said one day while he
was driving me to yet another fund-raiser and rally.
"But I would like to know what my birth mother was
like and why she gave me up and if I have sisters and
brothers somewhere. Maybe I have a sister somewhere who has the same color of eyes as I do or a
brother who walks just like me."

"I used to wish I had a brother or sister, mostly a
brother. They said that's why I had Nicky."

Rick glanced around at me. "Nicky? Who is this
Nicky?"

"Nobody," I said quickly.

"Should I be jealous?"

"Jealous?" My mind was whirring. "Nicky's not a boyfriend if that's what you mean. Are you?"

Rick laughed as he turned into the fairgrounds and found a parking spot. "You're a strange one, Erin."

"What do you mean by that?" I looked over at the fairgrounds. Mom's face was plastered on everything, and already people were milling about eating the barbecued pork chops and talking.

Rick didn't seem to notice the commotion at all as he answered me. "Maybe I should just say you're always surprising me."

"How?"

"You're just not what I expect. When I first saw you at school and found out who you were, I assumed you'd be Miss Socialite of the year. You know, popular, with lots of friends and everything. The perfect teenage girl."

"I have friends."

"Nobody real close. I've been watching you at school. You're nice to everybody with that constant, perfect smile of yours, but you don't really encourage anybody to get too close." He paused a moment before he added, "You haven't encouraged me."

"I didn't know you wanted to be encouraged."

"Well, now you do."

Everything outside the car faded away as we locked eyes. Inside I was quivering, wondering what to say next, and then I knew words weren't necessary. Rick traced my cheekbone with his finger.

After a minute, he said, "Who is Nicky?"

I pulled my eyes away from his and scrunched back into my seat. Again I heard the noise outside the car and saw the posters with the "Be a Winner with Winters" slogan.

"You wouldn't understand," I said at last.

Rick had never taken his eyes off me. "I might."

"No, it's all too strange. Even the doctors didn't understand. Not really. I'm not sure I do myself. Especially now."

"Who is Nicky?" Rick asked again.

"I'll tell you what they always told me. He's my imaginary playmate. Somebody I made up because I was a highly imaginative child and lonely at the same time. Nothing to worry about as long as it went away."

"And did it go away?"

"Not as soon as they thought it should. They began to suspect I was emotionally unstable. Mom, too, and I wasn't sure." I shut my eyes and remembered. "Everybody kept watching me, waiting for me to do something that would convince them one way or another."

"And that's when you started smiling."

I shook myself a little, opened my eyes and forced the smile across my face. "Of course not. I always smiled even before that."

Somebody pecked on the window, and I leaped at the interruption. "Jason," I said as I rolled down the window.

"What's taking you guys so long?" he said. "Grandmother sent me over here to get you. She needs more help on the food line."

"Go away, Jason," Rick said without looking at him.

"No, we're supposed to be helping." I pulled on the door handle.

Rick caught my arm. "I don't like it when you smile like that."

"Everybody else does." I pulled away from him.

"It's not real."

I kept the smile firmly on my face. "Yes, it is."

Jason stared at us. "Are you two fighting?"

"Of course not," I said as I got out of the car.

Jason looked over at Rick who was climbing out on his side. "I think you're fighting," he said.

Rick shook his head. "Who could fight with Miss Perfect here? See, she's smiling. That has to mean everything's all right, doesn't it?"

"Okay, but I still think you're fighting." Jason shrugged and started off between the parked cars toward the crowd on the fairgrounds.

Rick stepped in front of me. "He's right, you know. We are fighting, but I don't want to fight. I want to help you."

"I don't need any help."

"I think you do. I think you need to find out about your past as much as I need to find out about mine. Maybe more."

"I'm not adopted. I know about my past."

"Yeah," Rick said. "That's the reason you smile so much. Right?"

"Maybe it would be better if you smiled a little more yourself." I moved around him and on to the little group that surrounded Mom.

Later as I stood behind the food tables dishing out slaw, I was glad for the smile. It stood me in good stead even when I didn't feel like smiling.

Chapter Five

The rally lasted for hours. The smile got heavy, but I kept carrying it.

After the speeches and the handshaking and all the food was gone, people left. Mrs. Harris assigned Jason and me the task of picking up the napkins and cups scattered around the grounds.

Jason groaned, but I didn't mind. I was glad of the chance to move off by myself for a while where I could finally drop the smile.

It was late, and as the sun slipped close to the horizon, clouds caught its color and turned the sky a golden pink.

When the very air changed into rosy velvet, I dropped the trash I'd gathered and edged around to the back of the clubhouse out of sight. Once alone, I sank down on the grass and let the color flood my senses. My heart beat faster, and my fingers itched as my mind turned over combinations of colors that might capture some of the feeling of the sunset.

Then I was no longer alone. Nicky sat beside me, his eyes on the sunset. He'd come to share it with me, and because he had, the pinks deepened and began to glow.

My eyes swept over Nicky from the top of his blond hair to the bottom of his scuffed tennis shoes. His jeans were worn white at the knees, and he looked real and solid, not at all like a vision.

"Nicky," I whispered. "Where do you come from?"

Turning his head slowly away from the horizon to stare at me, he no longer looked so solid.

"Don't go away," I said softly, and he came back.

Somewhere in the distance, I heard someone calling for me, but I shut out the sound and concentrated on Nicky. "It is beautiful, isn't it?" I said.

He began to fade again, and this time I couldn't draw him back. Then when he was just a shadow in the air beside me, he said, *Rennie, help me.*

Even as I heard them, I wasn't sure if the words were in the air between us or only in my mind. Either way I was sure that Nicky had spoken them.

"Erin, what are you doing back here by yourself?" Rick asked as he came up behind me.

I put my hand down on the grass where Nicky had sat. The spot was cold. "Did you see anybody here as you came around the building?" I asked.

"I saw you out here goofing off while the rest of us were breaking our backs picking up trash."

"Nobody else?" I looked up at Rick.

"There's nobody else here, Erin. You can see that."

"Yes," I said softly. I shook myself a little. "I was watching the sunset. Did you notice the spectacular colors?"

"Sure," Rick said, but his eyes stayed on my face and away from the lingering beauty of the sunset.

"But I guess I shouldn't have quit working." I stood up. Nicky was gone. He wouldn't come back with Rick there. "Lead me to the trash bags."

"Jason and I have already finished. I just hunted you up to see if you wanted to go get something to eat."

"How can you think of eating after all the food we dished out this afternoon?"

"I don't know about you, but I never got a chance to eat any of it. I didn't know people could be so greedy. The way they were snatching and grabbing pork chops."

"That's the political system," I said. "Your vote for a pork chop."

"Some people didn't sell theirs that cheap. It was more like three or four. But I guess if everybody that was here votes for your mother, she won't have much to worry about. She'll win hands down."

"I hope so. She's really into this. If she doesn't win, I don't know what she'll do."

"She'll win. Me and you have a few weeks yet to see that she does. No telling how many pork chops we can dish out before the election." Rick grinned. "Speaking of pork chops, I'm hungry. Let's go."

Just before Rick and I went back around the clubhouse to where Mom's faithful Concerned Citizens group was clustered around her, I glanced back at the sky. The clouds were gray again with only a trace of color remaining from the glory of moments ago.

There was no trace of Nicky either. Yet his words still echoed in the back of my mind. *Help me, Rennie.*

"Something wrong, Erin?" Rick said when I stopped walking.

For a second, my gaze lingered on the empty air, but I couldn't chase shadows. "I guess I was just seeing things," I said and turned back to Rick. "Whatever, it's gone now. Let's go get those hamburgers, but hold the slaw."

Rick and I laughed and talked about the rally as we ate our hamburgers. He didn't mention Nicky, and neither did I even though his shadow hovered on the edge of my mind. How could I help him when I didn't even know what he was?

Each time the thought came to my mind, I shoved it aside. I could think about it later after Rick had taken me home. If I dared to think about it at all.

"I get the feeling every once in a while that you're not really listening," Rick said.

"Of course, I'm listening. You were talking about poor old Mr. Canton in his pink and green plaid suit and his work boots. But really, he's a sweet old man."

"I guess I shouldn't make fun of people. Every town has its weird characters."

"Brookdale may have more than its share. Sometimes I think I may be one of them."

"Don't be silly. You're not weird. Just artistic." Rick's smile was gone. "But you know, they could be part of my family."

"You don't really think Mr. Canton could be your father."

Rick thought about it for a minute before he shook his head. "No, but he might be an uncle or a third cousin. When I'm around a lot of people like I was today, I look at the faces and wonder if I could be looking at my mother and not recognize her. Or my father. It just seems like I ought to know if I was looking at the woman who gave birth to me, don't you think?"

"How could you? You never knew her."

"I knew her for nine months. She knew me, and she gave me away." Rick looked away from me. "And no matter why she did it, we ought to know one another."

"Can't you find her?"

"I'm searching. Mom's helping me."

"How about your father?"

"He doesn't like to talk about it much. I think he's afraid I might find out something that will hurt me, that it might be better to keep wondering instead of knowing that my mother was in jail or someone I might rather not be related to."

"You don't think she'd be in jail, do you? I mean really."

"I don't know. She could be anybody, anywhere. She could be the woman back there behind the counter taking orders."

"Mrs. Williams?" I looked at the dumpy, gray-haired woman who had worked at the Brookdale Grill ever since I could remember and couldn't keep from laughing. "Not Mrs. Williams."

"Why not?"

"She's got five kids and four grandchildren. But please don't ask her about the grandchildren. We'll be looking at pictures for an hour."

"Well, she might be a little old," Rick said after studying her a moment. "But somebody somewhere is my birth mother. Somebody who probably doesn't go around telling people that she's got a child somewhere that she gave away. Most likely it's a secret from the past, and that's another thing Dad keeps pointing out to me. He says my birth mother might not be very happy to see me.''

''I'd think she'd be as curious about you as you are about her.''

''But maybe not curious enough to risk upsetting her life now. She might never have told anybody about me, especially her husband and children, and I don't want to make trouble for her. I just want to meet her, to know something about where I came from. Some of the kinds of things you take for granted.''

''I can't help it if I'm not adopted.''

Rick smiled a little. ''Sorry. Sometimes I get carried away about it all.''

''You said you were searching. How?''

''It's not easy, but easier than it used to be. There are places that will put you in a computer to match you up with your birth parents. Of course, for that to work the birth parent has to be searching for you as well. I'm in two computers, but there's no match in either of them.'' Rick pushed back his plate and leaned back with a sigh. ''Sometimes I think it would be better if I weren't so healthy.''

''What's that got to do with anything?''

''When there's a medical emergency, it's easier to cut through the red tape to get the information you want. Say you've got a rare blood type or some kind of genetic disease."

"I don't think you should wish you were sick."

"I know. And Mom says we'll come up with a name one of these days or get a lead we can track down."

"You will." I tried to sound positive.

"I don't know. Things don't happen just because you want them to," Rick said.

"Sometimes they do."

Later when Rick took me home, Mom met us at the door and thanked Rick for all his help at the rally. Then after he'd left, she couldn't say enough nice things about him.

She went on about how good-looking he was, what great grades he made and how impressed she was by his hard work on her campaign. She ended by saying, "I'm glad you and Rick made up your argument."

"What argument?" I asked.

"Oh, Jason just told Evelyn that you two were fighting when you got to the rally this afternoon."

"The only way Jason would know a fight is if he saw it on his computer screen."

"Now, Erin. Jason's a sweet kid, a little bright for his own good, but he can't help that."

"If he was that bright, he'd know Rick and I weren't fighting." I headed for the stairs.

"Good," Mom said. "You and Rick make a cute couple."

Stopping, I turned back to look at her. "I don't know if we're a couple. He's just been hanging around with me because of the campaign."

"I think there's more to it than that," Mom said with a knowing smile.

"I like him," I admitted. "At least most of the time. Sometimes he goes out of his way to make me mad."

"Was that what he was doing today when Jason thought you were fighting?"

"Sort of."

"You want to tell me about it?"

"It was nothing really. He just likes to make fun of my smile sometimes." I put on the smile before I told Mom good night and raced up the stairs to my room.

Long after the house had settled into its late-night sounds, I sat up in the middle of my bed watching the moonlight sift through the window. I couldn't sleep. Too many voices were floating around inside my head with too many questions. Who is Nicky, Rick kept asking, and I still didn't have an answer even though I'd given him one. And then Mom saying Rick and I were a couple. Did I even want to be part of a couple? But the voice that kept sleep away was Nicky's voice asking me for help over and over.

Finally to shut out the voices, I flicked on my lamp and reached for my sketchbook. Turning to a blank page, I began sketching Rick. I pulled to mind the way his face had looked eager yet doubtful, too, while he'd talked about searching for his birth parents. The lines of his face were easy, and his mouth and nose came without too much effort. But his eyes were stubborn.

Erasing my light sketch marks, I tried again, but still the eyes were wrong. With my lamp tilted to give more light, I stared at the drawing before I erased the lines again. In my mind I could see the shape of Rick's eyes plainly. Why couldn't I transfer the thought to my pencil?

I erased and tried one more time. Still they were wrong. It was almost as if another person's eyes sat in Rick's face.

My hand grew still. Then slowly I turned back through my sketchbook to look at the other sketches I'd made of Rick. None of them were right, and now I could see why. Nicky's eyes stared out of Rick's face.

I flipped back to a clean sheet of paper and stared at the creamy white surface for a long time, almost afraid to make the first mark on it. Then hesitantly, I moved my hand across the page. The lines flowed without any conscious thought as Nicky formed under my pencil.

The scratch of the pencil was the only sound I heard as the rest of the world faded away. The lines came true and right the first time, and my eraser remained on the table.

At last I put down my pencil and stared at my sketch. Whether or not Nicky was real or just a shadow of my mind, I'd captured him on paper. The lines of his face were dark against the white of the paper, darker than I usually sketched because I rarely got the look I wanted the first try.

With Nicky it wasn't a question of getting what I wanted, but believing what I saw.

Reaching deep into my memory, I pulled forth the clearest image I could of the Nicky of my childhood. We'd been able to talk then, and Nicky was always laughing. Just thinking about it made me feel warm inside, and I picked up my pencil again.

Nicky's eyes wouldn't let me turn the page. So instead I drew the childhood Nicky in the lower corner of the same page. This time I used light marks and needed my eraser often, but when I was finished, the Nicky I remembered was staring up at me with his grin firmly in place.

My gaze shifted between the two sketches. If Nicky was just a product of my imagination, why had I changed him so much? The sketch of the child showed a face that was round and healthy. The new Nicky's face had stretched, become slimmer, but the real difference was in his eyes. The grin was gone, and even though I hadn't sketched in tears, they were there in the sadness that sat on every line of his face.

Rennie, help me. Were the words really there in the air of my room, or had I just imagined them?

I turned the sketchbook facedown on the bed and covered my ears. Still the sound echoed in my mind until I could no longer stand it.

Picking up the sketchbook, I stared down at the drawing of Nicky before I slipped out of my room and down the hall. When the floor creaked under my weight, I glanced toward Mom and Dad's bedroom. I didn't want to have to explain my being up in the middle of the night with my sketchbook under my arm.

With ghosts on all sides, I ran up the edge of the stairs, stepping over the steps I knew squeaked. The tower room was waiting for me, and I entered it gratefully. If I was ever going to figure out the mystery of Nicky, it would be here where he had once come so often to play.

The moon provided all the light I needed or wanted as I moved to the window seat and looked down at my sketchbook. In the gray light the sketch of Nicky was vague, hard to see, but the picture in my mind was clear.

So were the words. *Rennie, help me.*

"How?" I asked the shadows around me. "Tell me how." The sound of the words echoed in the empty room, and there was no answer.

As I stared out at the dusty moonlight, hearing the sound of my voice die away, I wondered if Mom was right. Maybe I did need to go see Dr. Carruthers.

When I woke, sunlight streaming through the windows had replaced the ghostly moonlight. For a second I didn't know how I had gotten to the tower room, and I wondered if I was still dreaming, if perhaps it had all been a dream.

Then I saw the sketchbook open on the floor where it had fallen out of my lap. Nicky stared up at me, and I knew that if it were a dream, it was a waking dream that wouldn't go away with the sunshine.

Stepping around the sketchbook, I kept my eyes away from Nicky's. As I crept down the stairs to my room, I hoped Mom and Dad were still asleep.

Once safely in my room, I pulled on some jeans and a sweatshirt before I tiptoed back through the hallway out to the porch. I wanted to feel the sunshine and watch it play among the red and gold leaves of the maples.

The fat Sunday paper was in the middle of the sidewalk. Sinking down on the porch steps, I opened it up to stare straight at myself on the life-style page. Mom, Dad and me, all smiling, all being the perfect family for the photographer and for the voters who would be reading about us over their morning coffee. They wouldn't be reading just about Mom, but also about Thomas, the supportive husband with a rich family heritage in politics who was a lawyer, and about Erin, the lovely daughter with the smile who was a budding artist. It was all perfect, exactly what the voters wanted to hear.

There would be no footnote that the daughter was seeing a psychiatrist. Whatever Nicky was, I'd handle it myself at least until the election was over.

Chapter Six

After church we mingled and talked with the rest of the congregation for a long time. I smiled and nodded a lot, agreeing with anything anybody said. I didn't find it hard to play the role of the perfect daughter. Nobody could tell by looking at me that I saw shadows and heard voices.

While we ate sandwiches and salad in the kitchen, Mom and Dad read the paper and laughed about some of the things the article said about us.

"But it is a good picture," Mom said.

"The perfect family," Dad added with a smile.

"Not really. There would have to be a son for that." Mom's voice went so flat that both Dad and I looked up at her.

"Not all perfect families have two children. Some of them just have one fantastic daughter." Dad smiled over at me. "Isn't that right, Erin?"

Mom pushed her half-eaten sandwich away from her and didn't say anything although Dad and I were both waiting for her to smile and agree with him. She didn't seem to know we were even there.

"What's the matter, Janet?" Dad asked after a few minutes.

Sighing, Mom rubbed her eyes. "I guess all this campaigning is just getting to me. Especially at church. Father would have never approved. But then I guess I've done a lot of things my father wouldn't have approved of."

"Not so many," Dad said mildly. "And besides you weren't campaigning at church. You were just being friendly."

"I was campaigning, and Father would preach a sermon against such a worldly use of his church grounds."

"Your father was firm in his beliefs," Dad said.

"Firm? They were in cement. He used to tell me all the time that I was an example for the rest of the church family to watch and see how a good girl should behave. Sometimes I felt as if little eyes were following me everywhere I went to catch me if I did anything wrong."

"Being a preacher's kid isn't easy, but you're exaggerating, Janet."

"I can barely remember Grandfather York," I said.

"You were only five when he died, and we didn't visit very often," Mom said.

"It was up in Ohio, wasn't it? I remember you used to buy me a new box of crayons every time we went."

Mom smiled, and some of the strain left her face. "Might know you'd remember the crayons."

"Rick's from Ohio, too," I said. "Did you know that?"

"I knew they moved here last year," Mom said as she got up to begin clearing the table.

"He wants to go back up there during the Christmas break to see if he can find some kind of record of his birth."

"Don't his parents have a record already?" Dad asked.

"Yes, but he's adopted, and he's looking for something that might help him trace his birth mother."

Mom turned from the sink to look at me with a little frown on her face. "You didn't tell me Rick was adopted."

"I didn't think it was important." When Mom kept staring at me, I added, "It isn't, is it?"

"No, of course not." Mom turned back to the sink. "Helen just didn't say anything about it."

"So he's looking for his biological mother," Dad said. "That's fairly common nowadays. If he needs it, I might be able to help him with some legal advice."

"I don't think that would be a good idea," Mom said without looking around.

"Why not? I wouldn't charge him anything, and it might be interesting. My case load is pretty light right now."

"I just don't think you should interfere in a personal family matter like that. Besides I need all the time you can spare to help me with the campaign."

"I wasn't talking about doing anything right this minute. Heaven only knows there's not time for anything but campaigning now."

"Even on Sunday," Mom said. "There's a function over in Whitesburg this afternoon."

Dad went up behind Mom at the sink and put his arms around her. "I'll drive so you can rest, and quit worrying about this Sunday campaigning bit. It'll all be over soon, and if your father wouldn't understand, then you can bet Grandfather would have. He's probably up in the attic now thumping his cane, telling you to get with it, that time's a-wasting, Sunday or not."

Mom let her hands rest in the dishwater and leaned back against Dad. "I always liked Grandfather Winters." Then she frowned again. "But what if I don't win?"

"You'll win. According to the latest polls Evelyn Harris quoted to me this morning, it would take a major catastrophe for you to lose now. Her grandson is keeping up with all the polls on his computer somehow."

"Catastrophe? What would you call a catastrophe?" Mom asked.

"Oh, that somebody found out that you were cheating on your wonderful husband."

"You're being silly, Thomas."

"Or that you'd come out for an increase in taxes."

"Nobody is supposed to mention that word until the election is over."

Dad laughed. "Grandfather must have been coaching you in your sleep."

I laughed too, glad that Dad was making Mom smile and forget her doubts. Watching them embrace made me feel happy, and then as I studied the shape their bodies made against the light coming through the window, my heart began beating faster. My artist's eye isolated and sharpened the merging lines of the scene in front of me until the unity of their shapes stayed with me even after Dad turned Mom loose and came back to the table.

They were talking to me now, and I had to force myself to retreat from the picture in my mind to listen.

"Do you want to come with us, Erin?" Mom was asking.

"Do I have to?"

"No," Mom said. "I just thought you might not want to be here alone all afternoon."

"You know better than that, Janet," Dad said. "Erin can't wait to get us out of the house so she can run up to her tower room and splash color around."

"I thought I might do some painting." I felt the eagerness growing inside me to have a brush in my hand before I lost the image in my mind.

After they left, I climbed the stairs slowly, letting the feeling of family unity build inside me. Everything that had ever happened in this house was connected by threads of family, some threads as thick as ropes, others as fine as spiderwebs, underlying everything we did.

I had never felt a painting so strongly as I began mixing the colors on my palette. Even the image of Nicky and the echo of his words that had been with me all through church and lunch faded into the background. There was nothing but me and the canvas with my brush the connecting thread.

When I faintly heard the doorbell ringing downstairs, I ignored it. But it kept ringing until my concentration, if not broken, was cracked.

Regretfully I put down my brush and climbed down the first flight of stairs. "Who is it?" I yelled.

"Erin," Rick called back. "Can I come in?"

"Just a minute." As I went on down the steps to the front hallway, my mind divided with part of it holding the image of my painting secure while the other part opened the door for Rick.

"Hi," he said. "I called but nobody answered."

"Mom and Dad aren't here, and I guess I didn't hear the phone. Were you wanting to know something about the campaign?"

"No, silly. I came to see you." Rick shifted his weight from one foot to the other. "I thought maybe you'd want to go for a ride or something."

"I can't today." The image in my mind was slipping, and I had to shift more of my concentration to holding on to it. Hardly realizing what I was doing, I began to shut the door.

Rick put out a hand to stop the door. "You wouldn't just close the door in my face, would you, Erin? I mean I thought we settled things yesterday so that you weren't mad at me any more."

"I'm not mad."

"What are you then?" He waved his hand in front of my eyes. "Are you even here?"

"Not entirely," I admitted. "I'm painting, and I don't want to lose my thought."

"So that's what's wrong with you. You're in your artistic mood." Rick studied my face a moment. "What are you painting?"

"If I talk about it, I'll lose it. In fact, if I keep talking period, I'm going to lose it. I've got to go back upstairs."

"If I promise to be quiet, can I come watch?"

"Why would you want to do that?"

"I don't know. I've never seen an artist at work before. It might be interesting."

"I doubt it, and I'm not sure I could paint with someone else in the tower room with me."

"You haven't stopped painting and you're down here talking to me. Somebody in the room with you won't hurt your concentration."

"I can't talk."

"Who wants to talk?"

"Well, okay, but it won't be interesting."

I led the way back up to the tower room where he settled down on the window seat without a word. For a few awkward moments, I felt his eyes on me, but then with the brush back in my hand, the connection was total again. I forgot Rick was there.

A long time later I stood back and looked at the shapes on the canvas. In my mind I still had the image firmly before my artist's eye, and in ways the shapes on the canvas matched it. In the center were the lines of Mom and Dad very close as they had been earlier that afternoon. All around them were other shapes with arms extended into threads as they reached out to one another. My shape was at the bottom of the picture, and all the arms came down to wrap around me. There beside me was another shape begging for connections but having none.

A shiver pushed through me as I stared at that lonely shape. Once again Nicky had entered my painting. Slowly, I began painting out the shapes, beginning with my own.

"What are you doing?" Rick asked from the window seat behind me.

I jumped and dropped my brush. I had forgotten he was there. "It's not right," I said as I picked up my brush and began slashing the painting with color again.

"It looked pretty good to me."

"Oh?" I kept painting the color on, covering the other shapes ruthlessly. "What did you think it was?"

"I didn't claim to know what it was. I just said it looked pretty good."

"It wasn't right," I repeated.

He didn't say any more until I had covered the canvas with color. With tingling fingers, I painted out Nicky's shape last, moving the brush up and down while inside I listened for a protest. There was none.

"It seems such a waste," Rick said softly.

As I stood back and looked at the blank canvas, the shiver ran through me again, and I dropped the brush and paints down on my work table as though they were hot. The color I'd used was the color of Nicky's eyes.

"What's wrong?" Rick asked, half rising out of the window seat.

"Nothing." I put on my smile as I turned to him.

"Don't smile at me like that," Rick said.

I kept smiling. "It's the only smile I've got."

"It's the only smile you've got when something's bothering you, and you don't want anybody to know about it."

"Are you sure you're interested in political science or psychology?" I turned away from him, but then my eyes caught on the painting again. So I had to look back at Rick. "Why don't we go for that ride you were talking about?"

"Why don't we talk?" Rick's eyes were steady on me as he held up my sketch pad. "Who's this?"

I stared at the picture I'd drawn of Nicky the night before, and my smile slipped away. Nicky's words began echoing in my mind. *Rennie, help me.* "Nobody," I finally managed to say.

Rick looked away from me down at the drawing he held. "He sort of looks like you."

In two steps I was beside Rick and had grabbed the sketch pad away from him. "Nobody said you could look at this."

"It was just lying there. I couldn't keep from looking at it."

"I should have never let you come up here."

"Why?" Rick stood up. "Are you afraid I'll get to know you? The real you, and not the person you pretend to be when everybody else is around? What are you hiding from up here, Erin?"

"I'm not hiding from anything. Some things are just personal and private."

"You're afraid."

"I'm not afraid of anything," I said as I stalked toward the door. "Least of all something I drew myself."

He caught up with me and grabbed my arm before I got to the doorway. "Who is that in the picture? Nicky?"

"Leave me alone, Rick." I jerked away from him.

"No, I won't. I want to help." He put his hand on my arm again.

"You can't. No one can."

"I can."

"What makes you so sure about everything?"

"I don't know. I want to help, but maybe I won't be able to. Maybe I just try to sound sure to cover up things I'm not at all sure about, just the way you smile to cover up things."

When I didn't say anything, he dropped his hand from my arm and turned toward the stairs. "I guess maybe I should leave."

"Wait," I said. "You're right. I am afraid."

Chapter Seven

I sat in the window seat, not saying anything as the sun wrapped its warmth around me. Rick leaned against the wall and waited. I was glad he hadn't left, but I still didn't know what to say, how to explain.

After a long time, he shifted on his feet and said, "Sometimes it helps just to talk even if there aren't any answers."

"You're sounding like Dr. Carruthers again," I said. "That's what she used to say. 'Just talk about it, Erin. Just talk about whatever is bothering you and I'll make it better.'"

"I don't know if I can make it better," Rick said.

"Dr. Carruthers couldn't either. Besides, there wasn't anything wrong then. I liked Nicky to come. It was only a problem for them because they couldn't figure it out...or me."

"Nicky, your imaginary playmate?" Rick picked up the sketchbook and flipped back through it, studying each page. "You know, you put his eyes in my face."

"I know. I didn't aim to."

"I'm not sure I understand about Nicky and this sketch." He pointed to the drawing of the little boy in the corner of the paper. "Is this how he looked when you used to play with him when you were little?"

"Yes. We always had fun." I smiled as I thought about it. "He liked to watch me draw, and sometimes he'd give me ideas for new pictures. He took one away with him once."

"What?"

I shut my eyes as I remembered. "I drew a picture of us together holding hands floating through the air. Nicky liked it, so I gave it to him. He took it away with him when he left."

"You can't give imaginary people things."

I opened my eyes and looked at Rick. "Exactly what Dr. Carruthers would have said which is why I didn't tell her about it. And I don't know. Maybe I did imagine drawing the picture, and that's why it was gone when Nicky left."

As if he didn't know what to say to that, Ricky looked again at the sketch. "Then this is how you imagine Nicky would look today."

"That's how he looks. Maybe I did imagine it, but not the way you mean. I've seen him. Whether he's real or not, I don't know." I didn't look at Rick. "He's everywhere."

"Is he here now?"

"I don't think so, but I can't be sure. He keeps showing up in funny ways."

"Like in your painting?"

"I won't even be thinking about him, and then there he'll be as though my paintbrush had moved on its own without any thought on my part."

"Do you think he might be a ghost?"

"No, he's not a ghost." I couldn't keep from laughing.

"How can you be so sure?"

"I don't really believe in ghosts."

Now it was Rick's turn to laugh. "You're sitting here telling me that this guy keeps appearing to you in all sorts of strange ways, you might even say haunting you, and he has to be some kind of spirit, yet you don't believe in ghosts."

"Well, I don't. Nicky's no ghost. Ghosts don't get older, do they? I mean if there is such a thing as ghosts, they would stay the same size, the same age forever, wouldn't they?"

"I don't know. I suppose."

"But Nicky grew up just like I did."

Rick stared down at the sketch of Nicky. "Has anybody else ever seen him?"

"No."

"Has he ever harmed you?"

"Of course not. Nicky would never hurt me."

"Then why are you afraid of him?"

"I'm not afraid of Nicky." I got up to go stare at the blue canvas. All at once I wanted to scrape all the blue off and have the shapes before me again so that I could draw my arms out around Nicky. I touched the spot where his shape had been. *Rennie, help me.*

When I turned to look at Rick, he was watching me. "Then what is it that you're afraid of?" he asked.

Over top Rick's words were Nicky's words. *Help me. Help me.* "Did you hear that?" I asked Rick.

"What?"

"He wants me to help him, but how can I help him when I don't know what he is?" I wiped the blue paint off my finger, and the echoing words stopped. When I looked up again, Rick was staring at me with an odd look on his face. "You think I'm crazy, don't you?"

He started to say something, but I rushed in front of his words. "Everybody I've ever told about Nicky has thought I was crazy. When I was a little girl, I never had any doubts. I knew I wasn't crazy no matter how many doctors I had to talk to. That's the reason I could play their games even when I hated it. But now I'm not so sure, and maybe that's what scares me.''

"I don't think you're crazy, Erin," Rick said softly. "It's just that I feel sort of that I'm in the twilight zone trying to deal with something paranormal like spirits or ESP. I've read up on all that stuff and weird things do happen sometimes.''

"I'm beginning to think you believe in ghosts," I said with a little smile.

"Just because I've never seen one doesn't make it impossible for anyone else to see one.''

"Nicky isn't a ghost. If he were, he wouldn't need me to help him.''

"But he's something, and that something isn't exactly normal or I miss my guess. Maybe it's like telepathy or something. I used to think maybe I could use that to find my birth parents, that maybe there was some weird connection of the minds that would give me a clue or at least make my mother want to find me.''

"Did it work?''

"I don't guess so. I haven't found her yet," Rick said. "But we're not worried about that right now. Right now we want to find out about Nicky.''

"He had on tennis shoes a lot like yours.''

"Then that proves he's not a ghost. Who ever heard of a ghost in tennis shoes?'' When I didn't smile, he went on. "Come on, Erin, smile. That was supposed to be a joke."

"You always tell me not to smile."

"But I like it when you really smile." He took my hand, and a smile crept up inside me. "Do you think maybe if we held hands like this I could see Nicky, too?"

"I don't know. I used to try to get Mom to see Nicky when I was little. I was sure she could have, but she'd never try."

"I'll try."

"I can't make him come. I never could."

"But you said he was here."

"Sort of. I keep hearing him, but it may only be in my mind."

"Are you afraid to let me try?"

"No." I held his hand tighter, taking comfort from the warmth of our clasped hands. "Listen then," I said as I reached out to touch the painting again. The words circled once more inside my head. *Rennie, help me. Help me. Help me.*

"Why can't you tell me more?" I demanded aloud, and the words fell off to a whispered murmur. I pulled my hand away from the painting.

"You heard him, didn't you?" Rick said, taking hold of my other hand and pulling me around to face him.

"You didn't?"

"No, but that doesn't mean I won't the next time. We'll just keep trying."

"You won't hear him."

"You give up too easily."

He still had both of my hands, and I looked at him shyly. "Thanks, Rick, for not laughing at me."

He let go of one of my hands, put his finger under my chin and tipped my face up until I was looking directly into his eyes. "I think I'm jealous of this Nicky," he said softly.

My eyes widened, and before I knew exactly how it happened, Rick's lips brushed mine. Inside my head, colors burst and spread like fireworks.

"Erin, are you up here?" Mom called.

I jumped away from Rick, but he kept a firm grasp on my hand. "Don't look so guilty, Erin. We weren't doing anything wrong," he whispered as Mom came through the tower room door.

Mom's eyes swept across my face, took in our joined hands and came to rest on Rick. "I thought that was your car out front."

"Rick wanted to watch me paint." Pulling my hand free, I moved a little away from Rick.

"It was interesting," Rick said. "I'd never seen an artist at work before."

Mom glanced at the blue canvas on my easel. "It doesn't look as if Erin did much painting."

"It wasn't right. I painted it out." I looked at Mom who was frowning. She hadn't been upset the last time I'd let Rick come up to the tower with me. Why now?

An odd, strained silence filled the tower room. Rick broke it by changing the subject. "How did your meeting go today, Mrs. Winters? My mother said it was an important one over in the next county."

"It went all right. They tell me I have the election locked in now. The two men running against me have split their following."

"That's great news, Mom, or should I say Representative Winters?"

"I guess we'd better wait till the votes are counted to be too sure of anything." Mom was still frowning, but her frown had nothing to do with the uncertainty of the outcome of the election. "Maybe we should go downstairs."

"I've got to be getting home," Rick said quickly. "I hadn't realized it was so late, and I've still got homework to do before school tomorrow."

We trailed down the steps behind Mom. At the bottom of the stairs, I said, "Why don't you stay and eat with us? We can fix some sandwiches."

When Rick hesitated, Mom spoke up. "You heard him, Erin. He said he had homework."

Rick glanced at Mom and back at me. "Yeah, maybe some other time, Erin."

I thought Mom would make some kind of excuse then and leave us there in the hallway alone so I could say goodbye to Rick. I even thought about him kissing me again, but Mom stayed rooted to her spot. So I followed Rick out the front door to his car.

When we were off the porch, Rick said, "I think she's mad at me."

"She's acting strange." I glanced back over my shoulder to see Mom watching us out the window. "She couldn't say enough nice things about you last week."

"It just surprised her, catching us like that." He touched my cheek. "It sort of surprised me too, but it was a nice surprise."

"Maybe we shouldn't have." I felt the pink glow of a blush bloom on my cheeks.

"What? Kiss?"

I nodded while my blush flamed brighter.

"I think maybe we should again as soon as possible," Rick said.

"I'd better go in," I said, quickly turning away.

He caught my hand. "Don't worry, Erin. It'll be okay. And don't worry about Nicky either. We'll find out who or what he is."

I watched Rick drive away before I went back into the house. I wished I could be as sure as he was, but I couldn't.

Mom was still in the hallway, waiting for me. I had the feeling she hadn't taken her eyes off me all the time I'd been out of the house, but now she wouldn't meet my eyes. "We'll have to talk about this, Erin."

"I thought you liked Rick," I said. She still had on her Be-a-Winner-with-Winters campaign button. The red button with white letters stood out against her navy campaigning suit.

"I do like him, but that doesn't mean you should let him come in when there's nobody home but you."

"We weren't doing anything wrong. He just kissed me. I'm old enough to let a boy kiss me if I want to."

The color drained from Mom's face. "I've been thinking, Erin. I do like Rick, but he is quite a bit older than you."

"Two years."

"That's a lot at your age, and I just don't think you're old enough to be getting seriously involved with anybody, no matter how nice they are."

"It was just a kiss, Mom."

"Kisses can lead to other things."

"Don't you trust me?"

"Trust has nothing to do with it."

I stared at her a minute before I lied and said, "I've got homework." I pushed past her to the steps.

"Don't you want any supper?" she asked.

"I'm not hungry."

At the top of the first flight of stairs, I started down the hall toward my room. Then when I heard Mom turn and go out to the kitchen, I crept up the stairs to the tower room.

Outside the sun was going down, but there was no sky full of colors tonight. Instead the sun was just slipping quietly behind the horizon without any fanfare at all. I watched the sky empty of the sun and the blue darken slowly as it embraced the night.

I looked around to see if Nicky was there to watch it with me as he had been at the fairgrounds, but the room was empty with not even a whisper of noise that couldn't be explained away by the wind. The silence fell heavily around me.

Though the light was fading rapidly in the tower room now that the sun was gone, there was still enough light for me to see the blue canvas. It was a study of silence. Absolute silence. I hadn't wanted the painting to be anything. I'd only wanted to make it blank again, ready for a fresh attempt at some thought inside my mind, but instead when I had painted it out, I had painted silence. Deep, complete, unwanted silence.

"I wasn't trying to shut you out, Nicky," I said softly. "I just don't know what you want me to do."

No answer stirred the air. Yet even as the silence deepened and became intense, I felt as though Nicky was trying to get through, but for some reason he couldn't.

The silence began to hum in my ears. With an effort I made myself move, pick up my sketch pad and escape the tower room.

Back in my bedroom, I turned on all my lights. Sitting on the floor under the brightest light, I quickly flipped past my other sketches and especially the sketch of Nicky to a blank page.

Line by line, I recreated the drawing I'd told Rick about that afternoon, the one of Nicky and me floating through a sky of clouds and rainbows and sunshine. It came whole, complete out of my memory and spread out on the page before me. I had drawn this once before, and I had given it to Nicky.

As I looked at the completed drawing, I knew what Dr. Carruthers would say about it. She'd say it was like a picture of Peter Pan, and that I wanted to escape reality by flying away into my imagination.

"Talk to me, Erin," she used to say. "Tell me what you don't like. Tell me what makes you so unhappy."

But I hadn't been unhappy except when the doctors poked and prodded at my mind. In time I had learned to hold tight to every image, concentrating on the shapes and colors to block out their words. I had told Dr. Carruthers about Nicky once, but she hadn't understood. She hadn't tried to understand because she already had him explained away in her mind. Her goal had been to make me accept her explanation.

Slowly I turned away from the sketch I'd just made back to the picture of Nicky. Lightly I traced around his eyes with my fingertip.

Chapter Eight

The next morning before I left for school, Mom told me that she thought it best if I stopped seeing Rick for a while. She and Dad had talked it over and decided I wasn't ready for a serious relationship.

I told Rick about it at lunch.

"I don't understand," Rick said.

"You don't understand? I'm totally lost. Last week you were the greatest guy she'd ever met. She was pushing me at you, talking about what a great couple we'd make."

Rick smiled and touched my hand gently. "Now that I can agree with."

Blushing a little, I thought about kissing him again right there in the middle of the banging forks and plates in the cafeteria. I looked at my untouched plate of food. "Anyway, this morning she's saying the exact opposite. It's as though she'd changed into a different person overnight."

"You looked too guilty when she came up to your tower room yesterday. No telling what she thought we'd been doing."

"That's not it." I pushed my green beans from one side of my plate to the other.

"Well, something must have happened to make her change her mind about me. Maybe I did something wrong in the campaign."

"No. She said you could keep working with the campaign if you wanted to, but that we just couldn't go off alone together."

"See, I told you. She thinks I'm going to attack you. She probably thinks I tried yesterday."

"You're being silly," I said.

"I'm trying to make you smile."

"Yesterday you told me you didn't want me to smile."

"We're talking about different smiles here. I don't want your Miss Perfect smile. I want the real Erin Winters's smile."

"I don't feel like smiling. I mean enough was wrong already without Mom acting like this." We were both quiet for a minute before I added, "I'd say it was because of Nicky, but Mom doesn't know I told you about him.''

"Nicky? Did you see him again?"

"No. He wanted to come, but he couldn't.'' I put down my fork and pushed my plate away. "I think he's sick."

"Don't worry, Erin. I'm going to help you. Together we'll find out who Nicky is."

"You can't help me. Mom won't let you come over any more."

"She'll change her mind again. I'll talk to her and tell her what a great guy I am, that she was right the first time and that I absolutely will not attack you. Scout's honor."

"I don't think it would help. You didn't hear her."

"Okay, tell me exactly what she said. It can't be as bad as you're making out."

I took a deep breath. "She says you're too old for me."

"I was this age last week, too."

"I know, and that I don't know enough about you and that I'm too young to get seriously involved with anybody."

"What makes her think we're seriously involved? Surely not one kiss."

"I let you come up to the tower room and showed you my paintings. I'd never done that before."

"You've never shown anyone your paintings?"

"Nobody but Mom and Dad and now you."

"I think I'm honored, but I also think you're hiding too much in that tower room. You should let a lot of other people see what you've done. Maybe have a show."

"I will when I'm ready."

"Will you?" Rick didn't wait for me to answer. "But that's another day's problem. Right now we have to figure out what's made your mother turn against me. Maybe somebody told her something about me."

"What?" I looked up at him.

"I don't know. That I was kicked out of school in Ohio or smoked pot. You know, that kind of thing." He grinned. "Not that any of it is true, but there has to be some reason for your mother's about-face."

"I don't think so. The only thing I've told her about you is that you were looking for your birth parents. We were talking about it at lunch yesterday before they left for the meeting. Dad said maybe he could help you with some legal advice."

"Then that's it." Throwing his napkin down in his plate, Rick climbed out of the bench to stand up. His face was hard, angry.

"What's it?" I asked, but Rick didn't answer as he grabbed up his plate and headed for the window. "Wait." I scrambled out of my seat to follow him.

He was halfway up the hall away from the cafeteria before I could catch up with him. Grabbing his arm, I jerked him to a stop. "Tell me what's the matter."

"It's because I'm adopted," Rick said flatly. "That's what made her decide not to like me."

"That's crazy."

"She's afraid I might have bad blood. She wouldn't want you to get mixed up with someone who comes from who knows where."

"Mom's not like that," I said.

"Yeah? You explain it then."

I couldn't think of a thing to say. I knew what he said wasn't true, but I didn't know what was.

"I think she just lost a vote," Rick said before he turned and went off down the hall. This time I didn't follow him.

Rick avoided me the rest of the day. That afternoon when I got home from school, Mom wouldn't talk to me when I tried to make her explain what she had against Rick. She just said she was doing it for my own good. In turn, I refused to go help her campaign.

After she left to meet Dad to go to whatever meeting was scheduled for that night, I climbed up to the tower room. The light was perfect, but I couldn't make any kind of brush stroke on the blue canvas.

I left the silence of the room and went outside to sit under the maples that Great-grandfather Winters had planted. The leaves had almost all fallen now, and were lying across the lawn in a thick carpet of pinks and oranges and yellows. There had been no time for raking what with all the campaign meetings and rallies.

Raking the leaves had always been a family chore and playtime as long as I could remember. Just smelling the leaves and hearing them crackle as I sat down among them was enough to bring a smile to my face. And Nicky used to come, too, before he went away. He had liked playing in the leaves, tunneling under them, hiding, and seeing if I could find him. Then after I'd found Nicky, I'd hide in the leaves with him until Mom found me. She had never known that Nicky was there.

Now there was no one here but me. I got the rake out of the garage and began pushing the leaves up into a great pile. The colors of the leaves mingled, caught the sunshine and reflected a pink glow. When the pile got too big to rake any more leaves onto it, I raked up smaller piles and carried them over to add to the great pile.

I was glad that the crackle of the leaves and the scratch of the rake against the grass shut out the silence.

When finally the pile was just right, I threw down my rake and jumped into the leaves. But it wasn't much fun playing in the leaves without someone to share them with.

I sat up in the leaves, and there was Nicky standing away from the pile watching me.

"Don't go away," I whispered. "Stay and play."

He shook his head slowly, sadly.

"You like the leaves, Nicky. You always liked the leaves. Remember, you said you didn't have any where you lived."

He almost smiled then, but still he was silent.

"Why won't you talk to me? You used to be able to talk to me, or did I imagine all that? Am I imagining this right now?"

Help me, Rennie.

"I don't know how," I practically shouted. "Tell me how."

As he began to fade, I reached toward him. I'd never touched him before even when we'd been children, but now I felt a hand in mine even as he appeared to be backing away out of my reach. Still there was a hand in my hand.

It wasn't until Nicky had faded away from my sight that I realized the hand wasn't his. Rick was beside me in the leaves.

I tried to pull my hand away, but Rick held it tightly. "I think I saw something, Erin," he whispered. "A shape, maybe a shadow—"

"I don't believe you," I said, staring at him. "How could you see something that's in my head?"

"Is that where it is? Are you sure?"

"I'm not sure of anything." I looked back at the spot where Nicky had stood. "But I think he's real. As real as you and me. And he needs my help."

"You have to find him."

"How can I find something I may just be imagining?" I pulled my hand away from Rick's and began piling the leaves one by one on top of my legs. "Do you think that if he's my other self, that I'll die if he dies?"

"What do you mean your other self?"

"He looks like me. His eyes are the same color."

"So lots of people are bound to have blue eyes in this world."

"The only other person I've seen with eyes the color of mine is Mom." I didn't look at Rick. Instead I studied the leaf I was holding.

"I like your eyes, but not just because of the color. I like your eyes because of how they see things and the way they look sort of mysterious as though you had secrets from the world."

"I do." Dropping the leaf I was holding, I picked out another one to study. It wasn't perfect either, and I discarded it for another one.

"Everybody has some secrets from the world."

I picked up another leaf. It was a beautiful reddish hue but ragged on the corner. I threw it aside and picked out a new one. "Do you?" I asked. "Have secrets, I mean."

"Sure." Rick picked up a leaf and studied it too.

"But my secrets aren't secret anymore. You know them."

"I'd share my secrets with you if I could, Erin, but my secrets are secret even from me."

I threw my leaf up so it could catch the wind before I reached over shyly to take Rick's hand. "Nothing you could find out about your birth parents could keep me from liking you."

"How do you know?" Rick crumpled the leaf he was holding.

"I know because it wouldn't make you any different."

"Your mother doesn't think so."

I took my hand away from his and began pulling the leaves up over me. I had given up looking for the perfect leaf. "I don't think that's why Mom said I couldn't see you anymore." I looked up at him. "I guess I'm disobeying her now."

"What will she do if she finds out?"

"I don't know. I always do what she says."

"Don't look so worried. She won't kill you, and some rules are made to be broken. Besides, you can tell her it was my fault. That it was my bad blood coming out."

"Don't say things like that." I wiggled my legs and watched the pile of leaves ripple up and down. "Besides I know you being adopted couldn't have had anything to do with Mom acting so weird. She must know somehow that I told you about Nicky."

"Why do you think she'd care about that?"

"I don't know, but she would. It used to embarrass her if I said anything about Nicky around one of her friends. She'd always cover it up by saying Nicky was our cat. She even got a cat and named it Nicky, but I called him Rennie."

"Why Rennie?"

"That's what Nicky calls me." I raised my knees up out of the leaf pile. "Did you really see him, Rick? Really?"

"It wasn't very clear, but I thought I saw something. Maybe I just *felt* it." He reached for my hand. "We could try again."

I let Rick take my hand again, and we sat there half covered with leaves while with each breeze more drifted down on top of us. Nicky didn't come back. I knew he wouldn't, but I hadn't said so because I wanted to hold Rick's hand.

After a long time, Rick reached out with his other hand and tipped my face around to look at him. "I want to kiss you again, Erin."

My heart seemed to stop and then begin pounding harder than ever as I lifted my face a little toward him.

The leaves crackled and crunched between us as he scooted closer and put his arms around me. Then with our lips touching, a soft warm glow of colors filled my mind. The glow stayed with me even after the kiss was over.

Rick reached up to pick a leaf out of my hair.

I thought then that he was going to kiss me again, and before he could, I jumped out of my covering of leaves and grabbed the rake. Rick stood up, too. "Here, I'll help you," he said as he took the rake from me.

We raked the leaves and hid their color in the brown of the garbage bags. We didn't kiss again although each time our hands touched as we filled one of the leaf bags, I thought about it and I think Rick did, too.

Chapter Nine

Mom and Dad came home from the meeting hours before I expected them. Neither of them said hello. Mom just stared at me while Dad hung up his coat and put away his briefcase.

"You're back early," I said to fill up the silence. "Didn't the meeting go well?"

"What's been going on here while we were gone?" Mom demanded without answering me.

"Nothing," I said. "I've just been trying to study my history." I held my book up off my lap a little.

"Nothing? Are you saying that Rick Lucas wasn't here?"

"I didn't say that."

"Then he was here. Evelyn Harris said she saw his car in front of the house." Mom's face was white.

"Take it easy, Janet," Dad said softly.

"Take it easy? We tell her she can't see Rick Lucas again, and then that's the first thing she does when we leave and you tell me to take it easy."

"You're getting too excited over all this, Janet," Dad said with a frown.

I closed my history book and sat up straight on the couch. "Rick was here, but I didn't ask him to come over. He just came. We didn't come in the house, and I didn't think it would hurt anything if we talked outside. We raked the leaves."

"You shouldn't have let him stay."

"Calm down, Janet." Dad tried again. "I don't see what it hurt for them to rake leaves together. He seems like a nice enough boy to me."

"We agreed that she was too young to get involved with him." Mom's voice was high.

"I don't think I ever agreed to that," Dad said quietly. "To tell you the truth, I'm a little confused about all this. What have you got against the boy, Janet?"

Mom didn't answer him. She turned to me. "We told you not to see him anymore."

"I can't not see him, Mom. We go to the same school." I looked up at her. "Besides I like him, and I want to see him."

Mom opened her mouth and then clamped it shut. Clasping her hands together, she turned to stare out the window at the dark.

Dad watched her a minute before saying, "I'm going to make us some hot chocolate so that maybe we can all calm down and talk about this sensibly."

With Dad gone, the silence built again. I wanted to break it, but I didn't know what to say. I'd never seen my mother like this. She was always in charge, in control, making things happen, but she was never unreasonable. Even about Nicky, she'd always tried to be reasonable.

I took one step toward her and then stopped when I noticed her reflection caught in the shadows on the window. The glass softened and blurred the lines of her features. I held the picture in my mind, a little ashamed that my artist's eye was working at a time like this and yet glad at the same time that I'd seen the reflection.

After a moment I pushed the image to the back of my mind and made myself say, "What made you decide not to like Rick, Mama? He hasn't changed since last week. Did somebody tell you something bad about him? If they did, it wasn't true."

Briefly her eyes came up to look at me in the reflection on the window. Then she dropped her head. "The issue here is not whether I like or dislike him, Erin," she said. "It's that you didn't obey me."

"This isn't a campaign with issues we're talking about. It's me. I'm sixteen. I'm old enough to have dates and boyfriends. You had dates when you were my age."

"Yes, but sometimes it was against my father's wishes, and I should have listened to him. I don't want you to make the same mistakes I did."

"I don't think Rick and me could be a mistake. We just sort of like each other. We're not planning to run away and get married or anything."

She sucked in her breath as though I'd hit her, and her whole body tensed. "I don't want you to see him anymore, Erin."

"You've got to give me a reason, Mama." When she didn't say anything, I went on. "Is it because I told him about Nicky?"

Mom spun around to face me. "What about Nicky?"

"I told him about how I used to play with Nicky when I was little and how I had to go to the doctors and how I hated it." I took a breath and plunged on. "Then I told him how I'd seen Nicky again just a few weeks ago."

"You said you dreamed that."

"Only because that's what you wanted me to say."

"It was a dream, Erin. It had to be."

"I don't know what Nicky is, Mama, but he's not a dream."

A shudder went through Mom, and she clasped her arms tightly around her body. "Maybe we should just move away from here, start all over some place fresh. I always thought I'd like to live in Colorado."

"Colorado? How can you talk about moving? The election is just weeks away."

"Maybe it was a mistake for me to ever run for office. Dr. Carruthers said the campaign might be what caused you to bring back Nicky."

"Maybe it's causing you to do strange things too, Mama. All this stuff about Rick is really weird. Last week we'd make a great couple and this week you're ready to move across the country if I keep seeing him."

I waited for her to explain, to start being sensible again, but she just looked at me. So after a few minutes, I plunged on. "Rick says it's because I told you he was adopted, that you think he might have bad blood or something, but I know that couldn't be it."

Mom turned away from me to stare at the window again.

"It can't be because Rick's adopted, can it, Mama?"

She didn't answer for a long time. Then she only said, "I can't talk about it anymore tonight, Erin. You'll just have to trust me to know what's best for you."

I stared at her while words rushed through my mind, but none of them made enough sense to speak aloud. The only thing I knew for sure was that Rick was right. Mom didn't want me to see him anymore because he was adopted.

I was still searching for something to say that would make sense when Dad came in from the kitchen with the tray of hot chocolate. He looked first at me and then Mom and then back to me. "Hot chocolate's ready. Come and get it," he said cheerfully.

At the window, Mom gave no sign of hearing him.

"I've got to finish my homework." I began gathering up my books and papers off the couch. "I'll go up to my room if that's all right."

"Sure," Dad said. "Take your hot chocolate with you."

When I picked the cup up off the tray, Dad touched my hand and whispered, "I'll talk to her."

I couldn't drink the hot chocolate. Hot chocolate was for good times, for building snowmen and sleigh riding and even late-night mailings. I couldn't remember ever drinking hot chocolate when things were wrong.

I pulled my eyes away from the steam rising off the hot liquid and tried to concentrate on the Spanish-American War. After I read one paragraph over four times without knowing what it said, I closed the book.

Staring out at nothing, I listened for the sound of Mom and Dad talking downstairs, but I couldn't hear even the murmur of their voices. A few minutes later, Mom came up the stairs and went into their bedroom.

Because I didn't know what else to do, I picked up my sketch pad. With hesitant strokes I drew my mother's face as it had looked in the window. Then I shaded it all over with a fuzzy gray before I held it at arm's length to study it. Her eyes were shadowed, evasive.

"Everybody has secrets." Rick's words rang in my mind. What was Mama's secret?

The house was silent around me, but it wasn't the comfortable late-night silence I'd always known. Something was wrong. Something worse than Nicky. Something about Rick.

I wanted to sneak downstairs and call Rick, but it was too late. I'd just have to wait and talk to him at school the next day. Maybe by then I'd be able to figure out what was going on enough to talk about it.

Even after I finally went to bed, I couldn't fall asleep. I thought about creeping up to the tower room, but then I remembered the blue canvas. I couldn't face any more silence. So I lay in bed and tried to think. When things got too jumbled up, I wiped all my thoughts away and started over. I felt as if I were in a maze, making the wrong turns over and over.

It was after midnight when Mom tapped lightly on my door. "Are you asleep, Erin?"

"No." I switched on my lamp.

"I couldn't sleep either. I thought maybe we could talk." She came in and sat on the side of my bed.

I pushed my pillows up against the headboard, leaned back, and waited.

Mom began working the edge of my blanket into pleats between her fingers. "I don't know where to begin," she said.

I wouldn't help her by saying a word.

"This campaign has been hard on us all. The meetings and everything. Don't get me wrong. I like campaigning." Mom let loose the pleats she'd made in the cover and glanced up at me for a second before she started folding the blanket edge again. "I guess it's my preacher father coming out in me. He preached the gospel, and I preach issues—people's issues."

"What's all that got to do with Rick and me?"

Dropping the cover, Mom got up and went to the window. I didn't try to see her reflection in the glass.

After a while, she asked quietly, "Do you know when Rick's birthday is?"

"No. He turned eighteen not too long ago, but I don't know the date."

"I should have checked the list of registered voters at the courthouse or asked Helen, and then I could have known for sure." Her shoulders sagged. "But maybe it's better I don't know for sure."

"I don't know what you're talking about."

"I know." She came back to sit on the bed, but she wouldn't look at me. Staring at the door, she began talking as though she were delivering a prepared speech. "When I was just a little older than you, I made a mistake. A bad mistake. I got involved with a boy I thought I loved, but as it turned out, we were both too young to know what love was about."

"Mom, Rick and I aren't doing anything we aren't supposed to do."

"You may be falling in love."

"We could be," I said. "I like him more than I've ever liked anybody except Nicky. Is that so wrong?"

"Let's forget about Nicky for the time being," Mom said.

"I'm not sure I can," I said softly even while the echo began in my head. *Rennie, help me.*

"I don't want to talk about that now. I want to explain why you have to stop seeing Rick and stop falling in love with him."

"I don't see what you have against Rick." I shut my eyes trying not to see Nicky's shadow at the window.

"Eighteen years ago I had a baby. A baby boy."

"You what?" My eyes flew open to stare at her.

She wouldn't look at me. "I told you I made a mistake, but it was a mistake nobody knew about except my mother and a cousin. Father would have disowned me.'' Mom took a deep breath. "I was young. The boy wouldn't marry me. It probably would have been a disaster if he had. Anyway, my mother shipped me off to her cousin in the northern part of Ohio. The cousin was supposed to be sick, and I went to take care of her. Father accepted the story.''

Mom's smile was sad as she looked around at me and went on. "He was so pretty. They let me hold him once before they took him away. I loved him, Erin, but I couldn't keep him.''

During the silence that followed her words, my mind grew still. In the distance I heard the normal night sounds of the house as it groaned with its age, but here in my room an intense circle of silence wrapped around my mother and me.

Mom spoke again, and though her words were soft, they jarred the silence. "So you see you have a brother.''

"And you think.'' I had to clear my throat before I could continue. "You think that brother might be Rick.''

"I don't know what to think. I just know it's a possibility, and I didn't know what to do about it.'' Mom rubbed her eyes. "Maybe I shouldn't have told you. I should have just checked into it somehow without letting anyone know. But when I found out he was adopted and the right age and from Ohio, I guess I panicked."

"It might not even be Rick," I said.

"It might not," Mom agreed. "But the more I thought about it tonight, the surer I was that I was going to have to explain to you why I'd been acting so strange."

"Does Dad know?"

"Not yet. I should have told him years ago, but I didn't. Now I'm not sure I can." Mom looked over toward the window, and I almost asked her if she could see Nicky but stopped myself in time. Mom was still talking. "He thinks it's the strain of the campaign that's bothering me."

Again silence hung in the air between us until Mom asked, "Do you think I'll make a good representative if I'm elected, Erin?"

"You know I do, Mom."

"But I won't win if the people find out I gave away my little boy. Maybe I shouldn't win."

"Don't be silly, Mom. What happened eighteen years ago isn't going to make that much difference to the voters now."

"You're wrong. The voters of this district are very conservative. They wouldn't forgive that kind of thing." Mom turned back to me. "But right now I'm more concerned about whether you'll be able to understand, Erin, and forgive me."

I wanted to reach out and touch her, but I couldn't. Even after her eyes filled with tears, I sat frozen. I couldn't remember ever seeing Mom cry, and she struggled to hold back the tears this time, too. She succeeded. Only one edged out of her left eye.

As she stood up, she attempted a smile and said, "I love you, Erin." Then leaning over, she dropped a kiss on my forehead. "I hope someday you'll be able to understand."

After she'd left, I still sat stiffly against the headboard, staring at nothing.

I had a brother, I kept telling myself, just as I used to wish when I was a little girl. I had wanted a brother so much.

I looked around for Nicky, but he had faded without a sound.

Chapter Ten

I didn't eat lunch the next day. I stayed in the library, pretending to study. When I caught sight of Rick in the hall, I turned before he could see me and went the long way to class. I got my first tardy.

I wanted to talk to Rick, but I couldn't tell him what my mother had told me. Not yet. And how could I stand there and talk to him as though nothing was different when he might be my brother?

Mom and I couldn't talk either. She kept sneaking looks at me, but she didn't mention our midnight conversation. Neither did I. There really wasn't time.

The Concerned Citizens group had arranged a debate between the candidates. I tried to beg out of going, but when I mentioned my load of homework, Dad told me in no uncertain terms that I could study in the car on the way.

"Your mother's feeling a little shaky about this whole debate, and she needs us to be there in the audience for support."

I kept my history book open on my lap during the ride. That way I didn't have to talk. Nobody said much as we drove over to the next county.

Once or twice Dad said something about the debate or the other candidates, but Mom barely mumbled in answer. I stared at the back of their heads and knew Mom hadn't told him yet.

The silence grew heavier, and I thought that if I was in the tower room I could paint us on the blue canvas. We would fit easily into that blue silence.

As we drove into the outskirts of the town, I began practicing my smile and running over my supply of stock answers. "Yes, I'm very proud of my mother." "I'm sure she'll make a wonderful representative." "No, I've never felt neglected because of my mother's political career. She always has time for me when I need her." "Of course, if I were old enough to vote, I'd vote for my mother."

I remembered Rick asking me once if I practiced in front of a mirror, and I wished I had a mirror to practice now. I needed to make sure my eyes showed a smile as well as my mouth.

Mom's smile looked a little practiced, too, as she took her place on the stage between the two other candidates. But as the questions began she seemed to forget everything but the issues at hand, and she spoke forcefully and convincingly each time the questions were addressed to her.

Once when one of her answers brought a wide scattering of spontaneous applause, Dad reached over and squeezed my hand. "She's great, isn't she?" he whispered.

Nodding, I smiled while at the same time Mom's eyes touched on me, and though her smile never wavered, I could see the worry in the way her eyes held on me for a second too long.

She looked so self-confident, so capable. No one would ever guess the secret she was hiding. I kept my smile firmly entrenched as I glanced around the room at the people. What would they do if they knew Mom's secret?

The first person I noticed was Evelyn Harris who was smiling and leading the applause. Would she withdraw the support of her Concerned Citizens group if she knew Mom had given a baby up for adoption eighteen years ago? Practically every member of the Brookdale City Council was in the audience to show their support for Mom. If they found out her secret, would it make a difference to them even after working with her for almost eight years?

Last of all my eyes caught and held on Helen Lucas. I was a little surprised to see her there. Mrs. Lucas must have felt my eyes on her because she turned and smiled across the gymnasium at me. I was glad my own smile was frozen on my lips.

Later, during a break, I found myself beside Mrs. Lucas. I tried to think of an excuse to disappear but came up empty.

"Your mother's doing well in the debate," Mrs. Lucas said. "She's so articulate and really has her issues well researched."

"Yes, I'm proud of her," I said with the smile.

"I told Rick he should come with me, but he said he had two tests tomorrow." She was smiling too, but she was also watching me closely.

"Really? I didn't get a chance to talk to him today at school."

"He said he didn't see you. He thought maybe you were sick."

"Just busy. I skipped lunch to study."

"Oh." Mrs. Lucas looked around. We had drifted off to the side away from the crowd. She hesitated and then said, "I don't mean to pry, Erin, but is there something wrong between you and Rick?"

I kept the smile firmly attached to my lips. "What do you mean?"

"Oh, I don't know." She looked uncomfortable. "I guess I shouldn't be asking you this. If Rick has a problem he'll come to me when he's ready, but he just looked so upset. And then when he wouldn't come tonight even though he knew you'd be here, well, I just thought maybe you knew what was wrong."

The smile faded, and I couldn't bring it back. "I'm not sure what's going on," I said. "Except that my mother has decided she doesn't want Rick and me seeing so much of each other."

"Rick hasn't done something he shouldn't have, has he?" Mrs. Lucas frowned. "He can be pretty headstrong about getting his own way sometimes."

"No, nothing like that," I said quickly. My face was flaming, and I wished I could have held on to the smile and stayed with the stock answers. "It's just all such a mess. He'll have to tell you about it."

Her face softened, and she patted my arm. "Well, I wouldn't worry, Erin. Things will no doubt work out for the best."

I didn't know what to say. Around us the murmur of the crowd began to settle as the candidates were finding their places on the stage again.

"Looks as though they're about ready to begin the second round of questions," Mrs. Lucas said. "We'd better find our seats."

As she turned away, I wanted to stop her. I wanted to blurt out and ask her if my mother could possibly be Rick's birth mother, but I clamped my lips together just in time to stop the words.

She stopped to speak to Dad. They both looked over to where I still stood rooted to the spot she'd left me. Dad motioned for me to come sit down because the debate was beginning again, but I mouthed the word rest room and escaped from the gym.

The rest room was empty. I was glad because I needed time to practice my smile before I had to use it again. After carefully putting the smile back on my face, I quietly went back out to slip into my seat beside my father.

I didn't even try to listen to the questions and answers of the debate now. I just sat there with my smile hiding the secrets I knew and wondering about the other people in the crowd. Did they all have dark secrets, too?

My mind grabbed at the idea, and I watched first one person, then another as I tried to guess what their secrets might be. I imagined each of them with a shadow lurking over or behind them, a shadow no one else could see but that they knew was there all the time, just as Mom had lived for years with the shadow of her other child.

I had a shadow, too. Nicky was my secret. And now I had the burden of sharing Mom's secret as well.

On a dark canvas in my mind I began arranging shapes and shadows. Even after the debate was over and people started talking to me again, I managed to hold on to the shape of the secrets. It took very little thought to give the answers I had ready to the same questions I was always asked.

I pretended to be asleep on the way home so that I wouldn't have to talk. There was nothing to say anyway. People didn't talk about their secrets. It was too hard.

The next day at school I avoided Rick again. When I got home, I went straight up to the tower room. Sitting in the middle of the floor with the fall sunshine warming me, I sketched the shadows of secrets I'd imagined the night before.

Twice the phone rang, but I didn't move to answer it. In fact, I barely heard the ring. It was as if I had removed myself from the real world and had entered into the shadows I was sketching. The world of Nicky.

When my hand began to cramp from drawing so long, I leaned my head over on my knees and called to Nicky. I wanted him to come back. But even his cry for help stayed away.

I didn't remember ever feeling so alone, and this time when the phone started ringing two floors below me, I didn't have any trouble hearing it. Still I didn't move as the sound echoed up the stairs to me.

When the rings finally stopped, I turned the sketch pad back to the picture of Nicky and stared at it until the sun no longer came through the tower windows. Had he ever really been here or was he only a figment of my imagination?

I wanted him to be real, not just something I'd imagined because I was lonely. It didn't matter that there was no way he could be real. No logical way. Dr. Carruthers had told me so hundreds of times. Maybe all these years later I was finally going to have to accept what she said as the truth.

Although I went to bed as soon as it got dark, I heard Mom and Dad when they got home much later. Mom peeked in at me, but I stayed still under my covers. So she left without saying anything.

Later as I was drifting off to sleep, I thought I heard the tower stairs creak, but then I decided it must have just been the house settling. Nobody ever went up to the tower room unless I was there.

The next morning I tried to wait till the last minute to go downstairs so I could just yell goodbye and run, but Mom had other ideas.

"I'll take you to school, Erin," she said as she stood up from the table.

"That's okay. I can walk."

"It looks like it might rain, and besides I need to talk to you a minute before we go."

"I haven't seen Rick anymore," I said.

"I know." Mom poured the rest of her coffee down the drain and then rinsed out her cup. She leaned against the sink a minute before turning back to me and saying, "I went up to the tower room last night."

"Oh?" I said while inside I grew still. The hum of the overhead fluorescent light sounded loud as I waited for her to go on.

She looked all around the kitchen and finally at me. "I looked through your sketchbook. I mean you've never said I couldn't."

I thought over the sketches I'd made in the past weeks. "Well, they aren't anything special," I said even as I was thinking that I should have hidden the book.

"Actually I think they're probably very good, Erin, but they scared me."

"They're just sketches." The hum of the light grew louder.

"They're so dark and depressing. So sad."

"I've always liked drawing shadows," I said.

"These are different. You know yourself they are. Even that solid blue canvas you have up there is depressing."

"It's silence," I said.

"Oppressive silence," Mom said with a little shudder.

"Not all the sketches are depressing. I drew some of Rick, but they weren't very good."

"Yes, I saw them. And the other boy?" Mom looked down at her hands. "Is he Nicky?"

"Yes." I listened hard inside my mind for the echo of Nicky's cry for help, but the silence rang that much louder. Maybe he was dead and that was why I couldn't hear him any more.

"I talked to Ellen Carruthers last night. She's going to arrange for us to see a Dr. Hopkins as soon as possible. Maybe tomorrow."

It took a few minutes for me to realize what she was saying. "I won't go."

"We're both going."

"No," I said, meeting her eyes. She looked away. "Besides, how would it look for the daughter of the front-running candidate for state representative to be seeing a psychiatrist? That would make really good reading for the opponents."

Mom almost smiled. "I guess it'll look worse for the candidate to be seeing the psychiatrist, but I'm going, too."

"Why? You're not seeing things."

"I told Ellen everything last night. I never did when you were little, you know. I didn't see how the baby I couldn't forget could have anything to do with you, but Ellen thinks we could have some kind of strange telepathic connection and that maybe that's why you kept thinking up a big brother."

"That's crazy."

"Maybe, but nothing about Nicky was ever too sane."

"I won't go," I said again.

"And I won't sit back and do nothing while you slip away into a world of shadows."

"I'll draw flowers and rainbows if that will make you happy," I said.

"It's you I want to see happy."

"I'm happy." I pulled on my brightest smile.

Mom shook her head sadly. "That's your political smile. Surely, Erin, you know that I can tell the difference."

"I'm going to be late for school."

Without another word, Mom grabbed her coat and purse and followed me out the door. As we were backing out of the drive, I looked back at the house. The morning was cloudy, and the windows of the house were gray, hiding all the shadowy shapes behind their panes.

My eyes traveled up to the tower windows. We were pulling out into the street when I thought I caught a glimpse of a face in a tower-room window, and I had to force myself not to grab the door handle. I wanted to run back into the house and up the stairs to see if it really was Nicky. I wanted so much for it to be Nicky because that would mean he wasn't dead and that there was still time to help him.

But I held my hands tightly together in my lap and let Mom take me on toward school. I was afraid if I said anything she might just drive past the school on toward the doctors. And maybe I was slipping away into the shadows for when I looked back again the window was empty.

Chapter Eleven

That afternoon when I got home from school, Rick was sitting on the front steps. I hadn't seen him at school, but then I'd been in a kind of daze all day.

I didn't want to go to the doctors, but I didn't know any way to get out of it. I kept telling myself that maybe I'd like this Dr. Hopkins better than Dr. Carruthers. And so the argument had gone in my head all day as if I were plucking the petals off a daisy. She's going. She's going not.

Now here was Rick on the steps, and I wasn't going to be able to put off talking to him any longer. I looked at him and then quickly away even though

I wanted to search his face. Surely if he were my brother, I'd be able to tell.

"Hi," I said with my brightest smile.

"Don't smile at me like that." His voice was almost a growl.

"Sorry." Letting the smile slip away, I hugged my books up against me and stared at the ground.

"You've been avoiding me at school."

"No, I haven't. I've just been busy."

"Come on, Erin," Rick said. "We've got enough problems without lying to each other. You haven't eaten lunch all week, and you've been running the other direction every time you see me in the hall."

"Mom said I couldn't see you anymore."

"I don't think she would have minded us saying hello in a crowded hallway between classes."

I still didn't look at him. "I thought it would be better if I didn't see you at all."

"I know what you thought," Rick said.

I shifted my eyes from the ground to the tower windows high above us. They were empty. After a minute, I said, "How could you know? I'm not sure I know myself."

"I talked to your mother."

I couldn't keep from looking at him then. "When?"

"She came to school and pulled me out of last period. I guess there are advantages to being mayor of the town. The principal couldn't wait to see me out the door with her.''

"I doubt if he thought she was trying to kidnap you.''

"I wasn't sure what she was planning to do with me, but I'm glad I agreed to go with her. I guess she won a vote back.''

"Mom's not one to let a vote get away from her.'' I dropped my eyes back to the ground. My heart was beating in my ears, and I felt a little sick.

Putting his fingers under my chin, Rick lifted my face up until I was looking into his eyes. "It's all right, Erin,'' he said softly. "She's not my mother.''

"She told you that?''

"No, I guess I told her that. The birth dates didn't match up. I don't know whether she was more disappointed or relieved.''

Relief sprang up inside me like a bird taking wing. "I'm glad you're not my brother.''

"Yeah, well, it would have taken some adjustment on my part, too.'' Rick grinned.

"I still can't believe she told you.''

Rick's grin disappeared. "She had to know for sure one way or another.''

"But she thinks if anybody finds out that it'll cost her the election. I didn't think she'd take that chance.''

"The election's important to her but not as important as you. She's worried about you, Erin.''

"I know." I dropped my eyes to the ground again. "She looked at my sketchbook, and now she thinks I'm losing my mind. There weren't any flowers and rainbows."

"She told me."

"I don't think I like her discussing my problems with you."

"Why not? She's just trying to find a way to help."

"She thinks the doctors will help." I looked out toward the maple trees where already the ground had a new covering of bright colored leaves. Maybe if I raked leaves again, Nicky would come back.

"Maybe they will," Rick said.

"I'm not the one who needs help. Nicky is, and nobody can help him but me."

"Your mother doesn't understand that." Rick paused a minute, and I could feel his eyes on me. "And I have to admit that I'm not sure I do, either."

"I don't have to understand it. I just know it's true. The same as I know that I just can't go back to the doctors and go through all that again. They want to change the truth, make it a reasonable, sane truth that makes sense."

"What is the truth, Erin? Who do you think Nicky is? Or what?"

I watched the wind shake loose more of the maple leaves, and I listened hard as they fell toward the ground to see if I could hear them land.

After a few minutes, Rick said, "You can't just shut everybody out. You have to talk about it."

"I don't think talking will help."

"You told me about it."

"I probably shouldn't have told you, and I know I shouldn't have told Mom."

"But you did tell us, and now you have to let us try to help." When I didn't answer, he said, "Can I go up to the tower room with you?"

"Why?"

"Do I have to have a reason?"

"No, but I think you do." I glanced at him and quickly away. My eyes were running out of things to look at, and I wished my artist's eye could catch on an image so I could concentrate on that and not have to think. But there was nothing but Rick and me standing on the steps with Mom's shadow over us. Though she wasn't there with us, her words were.

"What reason do you think I have?"

"My mother. She's convinced you to try to talk me into agreeing to go to the doctors."

When he started to deny it, I cut him off. "You just told me that we shouldn't lie to one another."

"Okay. I want to see these sketches that have upset your mother so much, and I want to look at your drawings of Nicky again."

"Maybe you should just go home." I started up the steps toward the door.

Rick grabbed my arm and stopped me. "What are you afraid of, Erin?"

"Nothing," I started.

Rick didn't let me finish. "The truth, Erin. Remember we're telling each other the truth."

"Maybe that's what I'm afraid of. The truth."

I let him follow me up the stairs to the tower room where I handed him the sketchbook without a word. Then I turned away from him to stand by the window where I had thought I'd caught a glimpse of Nicky that morning. Not even an echo of him was there now.

Behind me, I could hear Rick flipping the pages of the sketchbook.

After a long time, he said, "Have you ever been happy, Erin?"

I turned from the window, but Rick didn't look up from the sketchbook. I tried to explain. "Just because I draw shadows doesn't mean I'm not happy. The artist in me just draws what she sees. It doesn't have that much to do with me. Can you understand that?"

"I don't guess anybody is supposed to be able to understand the creative mind." He flipped back through the sketches. I couldn't see the drawing he was staring at, but I knew it was Nicky. He said, "And this stuff with Nicky. Is that just the artist in you, too?"

I went over to look over his shoulder. Nicky's eyes seemed to speak to me out of the drawing. "I don't want him to be just my imagination. I want him to be real. Maybe that's why I always hated going to the doctors. Maybe that's why I don't want to go to the doctors now."

"Have you seen him since the day we raked the leaves?"

"He came that night while Mama was telling me about the baby. But now he's gone."

"Were you ever able to call him, to make him come when you wanted him to?"

"I'm not sure. I can't remember exactly how it was when I was little. It was just so natural then, sort of like laughing. If the time was right, he came."

"Do you want to call him now?"

I sat down by Rick on the floor. "It won't work."

"Are you afraid to try?"

"Sort of," I admitted. "You know, Nicky was a strange but good part of my childhood. I'm not sure I want to know what he is."

"But he's haunting you. I mean you can say what you like about the artist in you, Erin, but I can see how the dark shadows are taking over since I first looked at your paintings. I don't blame your mother for being worried. I'm worried, too."

"Then you think I should go to the doctors." I ran my hands slowly across the wooden floor, my fingers leaving tracks in the dust.

Rick laid the sketchbook aside still open to the sketch of Nicky. He answered carefully, "I think you should face whatever it is and not let it just haunt you."

"That's what you would do, isn't it? That's the way you want to do it with your birth parents."

"I believe it's better to know the truth."

"Even when that might be something you'd rather not know?"

"If it's the truth, I'd rather know it and face it and go from there."

"Maybe you're just saying that because you haven't had to face the truth yet."

"You don't have to do it if you don't want to," Rick said. "You can just keep living in a shadow and wearing that fake smile of yours. You could probably even go to the doctors and fool them all again."

I looked over at the windows again. "All right. I'll try to call him, but I don't think I can."

Rick took my hand and clasped it tightly between his without saying anything else.

Time passed. I didn't speak Nicky's name aloud. I just let his name echo through my mind the same way his call to me had echoed through it.

Nicky. Where are you?

No answer came. My eyes strayed around the room until they caught on the blue canvas. The silence was terrible, suddenly more than I could bear.

I jerked my eyes away from the painting and my hand from Rick's. "I can't," I whispered. "I can't."

"It's okay, Erin." Rick put his arms around me. "You don't have to try."

"I did try, but he won't come." I looked back at the blue painting and then quickly away. "Something's wrong. I don't think he's coming."

Rick's arm stiffened against my back.

Pulling my legs up close to me, I leaned my head over on my knees. "I know this all sounds crazy, and I don't blame you for not believing it. I don't know that I believe it myself."

Rick's arm came back around me. "I believe you, Erin. I just don't understand."

"Who does?"

Rick was quiet for a long time before he said, "Maybe your paintings are your link, Erin. Maybe they're the key to solving the mystery of Nicky."

"You're sounding more and more like Dr. Carruthers. 'Draw your dream, dear, so we can pull it apart and see why you're so weird.'"

"Did you ever draw Nicky for them?"

"No, but Mom took in some of the drawings I did at home." I picked up my sketchbook. "Maybe I should burn these before I start the doctors again."

Rick took the sketchbook from me and began flipping through the pages. He stopped at the sketch of Nicky and stared at it a moment before he said, "Your mother was telling me about this doctor you used to go see, Dr. Whatever you said her name was, and that she had this theory that maybe you and your mother had some kind of weird telepathic link."

"She told you everything, didn't she?"

"It's an idea that makes a strange sort of sense." Rick laid the sketchbook down on the floor in front of him. Nicky stared up off the paper at us. "I mean this picture is so real."

I touched the lines of the sketch, remembering how easily they had come from my pencil. "This picture was sort of given to me."

"What do you mean?"

"Some sketches are hard, but then occasionally there'll be a sketch that will come so easily that it's like a gift. This one of Nicky was a gift."

Rick looked at the sketch, then up at me. "You're going to have to tell your mother about all this, you know."

"I can't."

Rick took both my hands in his. "Erin, the only thing you can't do is keep hiding behind that perfect-daughter, perfect-girl pose. You've got to be the one that makes things happen. You've got to make the first move."

"Why?"

"Because you're the only one who can."

"No." I tried to pull my hands away, but Rick held tighter. So I sat still and let him hold my hands, but I looked out the window toward the sky. "No," I repeated. "I'll go to this Dr. Hopkins and tell him what he wants to hear and then it will all be over again just the way it was the last time."

"You can do that. You can smile your perfect smile and pretend that everything is perfect and they'll probably believe you." He waited a minute before he added, "But it wouldn't help Nicky."

My eyes flew away from the sky back to his. It took a minute to form the words out loud. "Then you believe there is a Nicky?"

"Of course. And now we know who he is."

Chapter Twelve

Rick wouldn't stay till Mom got home even though I begged him to.

Instead he gave me a little hug and stood up to leave. "You're the one who has to tell her, Erin."

"She won't believe me." I stared down at the dust tracks my fingers were making on the floor.

"Show her the sketches of Nicky."

"She's seen them already."

"Show her again."

"It won't make any difference. I won't be able to make her believe it."

Squatting down in front of me, Rick lifted my face up. "Yes, you will, because you know it's true. You've always known Nicky was real, haven't you?" Without waiting for an answer, he dropped his lips softly down on mine. "I'll call you later," he said then and was gone.

I listened to him lope down the stairs. After the door banged shut behind him, silence settled heavily around me.

When the silence grew too loud, I picked up my pencil and began drawing. Nicky's shape formed on the page under my hand almost without conscious thought. Again the lines were a gift, and I finished the sketch quickly.

Then when I held it up to look at what I'd drawn, I shuddered. In the sketch Nicky was lying down, his eyes staring up at a dark shadow hovering over him.

Daylight crept slowly out of the tower room, but I kept staring at the sketch long after I could no longer see the lines on the paper. I didn't need to see Nicky with my eyes.

By the time Mom and Dad came home, I knew Rick was right.

Mom climbed up to the tower room where she hesitated in the doorway. "Erin?"

"I'm here," I said.

When she switched on a panel of lights, I shielded my eyes from the sudden brightness.

"Are you okay?" she asked.

"I'm okay. I was thinking."

"In the dark?"

"Sometimes that's the best place for thinking."
Slowly I got up, stretching to get the kinks out of my
legs. "Where's Dad?"

"Downstairs in the kitchen."

"Have you told him?"

"I told him," Mom said softly.

I looked up at Mom who had stopped just inside
the door. Even the crisply pressed campaign suit
couldn't hide the droop of her shoulders, and she
looked even sadder than she had the night she'd
stared out the window while the secret was still hers
and hers alone.

I pushed out the words. "Is everything okay between you and Dad?"

"We'll work it out." Mom looked beyond me toward the windows. "It's just that he can't understand why I didn't tell him years ago, but I didn't
want to spoil things between us. And I always
planned to tell him later. There was just never a good
time."

"Now wasn't a good time either."

"No." She took a deep breath and looked at me.
"I talked to Rick today. He's not your brother."

"I know." I met her eyes, eyes the same color as
mine and as Nicky's. I looked from her to the
sketchbook. *Help me, Rennie.*

"Rick's not my brother, Mama, but somebody is."

"Don't you think I know that, Erin, but wherever he is he has a life separate from me. I gave him up years ago, and I can't try to reclaim him now. It wouldn't be right." Mom shook her head while she spoke. Then she added, "We just have to forget about him again."

"I don't think we can." I held out my new drawing of Nicky. "Rick thinks Nicky is my brother. He thinks the telepathic link Dr. Carruthers was talking about between you and me is between Nicky and me instead."

Mom was only half listening as she stared at the sketch. "Why did you draw this, Erin?"

"I don't know."

"I don't like it." Mom looked up at me.

"Neither do I, but I had to draw it."

"You're scaring me again."

"It scares me, too." I hesitated a second before I went on. "If you want to call that Dr. Hopkins, I'll go see him whenever you want me to."

"I'm not sure he could help us." Mom's eyes were fastened on the sketch again. "We'd better go talk to your father."

Down in the kitchen, Dad was sitting at the table staring at his hands. He didn't look up when he heard us. Mom stopped just inside the kitchen door the same way she had in the tower room. I edged past her to the sink. I saw how the space was pushing us apart, and even while I wanted to draw us all closer together somehow, my artist's eye was coldly clinging to the image of us apart. I wished I could shut it off, not let it see, but I could not.

Mom waited for Dad to look up and say something, but when he didn't, she straightened her shoulders a bit and moved briskly over to the table. "We've got to talk, Thomas."

When he still didn't say anything, she went on. "Not for my sake, but for Erin's." Mom pushed the sketchbook across the table at him. "Here, look at this."

After a minute Dad began leafing through the book. Once he paused and glanced over at me before he turned to a new page.

"They're very good, Erin," he said finally.

"But disquieting," Mom added.

"Who is he? I mean I recognized Rick, but who's the other boy?"

"Nicky," I said.

"Nicky? Wasn't that the name you gave your imaginary playmate when you were little?"

"He's my brother, Dad, and we have to find him. I think he's dying."

Dad looked from me back to the drawing and then up at Mom. "I think you'd better start at the beginning."

And so I told him about Nicky coming back, and Mom explained Dr. Carruther's theory about our telepathic link.

"It's all crazy," Dad said when we finished. "Neither of you is making sense, and while I can understand that with Erin—she's always had flights of fancy—I can't see you believing all this, Janet."

Reaching over, Mom scooted the book back to her side of the table. She riffled through the sketches. "There was always something about Nicky that bothered me," she said softly, staring at one of the drawings. "Maybe that's because he's the child I deserted."

"You did what you had to do." Dad reached across the table and took her hand. "Now you have to forget it."

"No." Mom still stared down at the sketch. "If this is my child, I won't desert him again."

"But what can you do?"

"Find him."

Dad pulled his hand away from hers and rubbed his forehead. "It's crazy, Janet. The election is only a little over a week away. You know what the papers will do to you if they get hold of this story."

"I'm going to make a statement to the press tomorrow."

"They'll eat you alive."

"Perhaps, but it has to be done."

Dad glanced over at me. "Well, if you won't think of yourself, think of Erin. They'll be merciless if they think this has to do with some kind of weird psychic ability on her part. It won't matter whether it's true or not."

"I am thinking of Erin, and there'll be no need for any of us to state why or how we found Nicky."

Dad thought for a moment before he said, "I can go along with that. Then why don't we wait till the election is past? One more week can't hurt after all these years."

Mom looked up at him. "It might."

Getting up from the table, Dad paced around the room twice before he took a pan out of the cabinet, put it on the stove and began rummaging in the cabinets.

"What are you doing?" Mom asked.

"Fixing hot chocolate. Maybe it'll help us think so we can figure out exactly how we're going to find this boy."

"Thank you, Thomas," Mom said solemnly.

He met her eyes, and though they didn't touch there was every bit as much closeness in that look as there was in a dozen hugs. I wished for my pencil to sketch the feel of that moment so I wouldn't forget it. Then I knew I'd never forget anyway. Whenever I wanted, I'd be able to call back the power of that image whether it was in two days, two months or two years from now.

The next day Mom gave a statement to the press. She told them that she had become aware of the adopted child's need to know about his ancestry because of an adoptee who was working in her campaign. She told them that since the child she had given up for adoption was now eighteen she had decided that he, too, might be searching for his birth mother.

Dad and I stood on the platform behind her as she spoke. Though I couldn't see her face, her voice sounded strong and confident.

When one of the reporters asked her why she was revealing this information now instead of after the election, she answered without hesitation. "I believed the voters had the right to know before they cast their ballots in the election next week."

"Do you think it will cost you the election?" a voice called from the back of the group.

"The people of this district are the finest people in the world, and I think they will be understanding. More importantly, I think they care enough about the government of this district to decide the election on the issues raised in our campaign." Given this perfect opening, Mom launched into a short but powerful speech about what she would do for the district when elected.

When she stepped down from the platform, a scattering of applause accompanied the flashing of the cameras. Glancing around to see who had started the clapping, I caught a glimpse of Rick and his mother at the back of the crowd. Then Martha Long, a reporter for the biggest newspaper in the area, grabbed me as I stepped down behind Mom.

"What do you think about all this, Erin?"

"I'm proud of my mother," I said quietly, but I didn't smile at the woman who had cornered me.

"I mean knowing you have a brother. When did you find out?"

"I've always known," I said calmly.

"Why did your mother pick now to announce it?" the woman asked, holding her recorder up to catch my answer.

"She told you," I said.

"You mean all that stuff about the voter's right to know? That's political talk, dearie. Come on now, Erin, and give your old Aunt Martha a scoop and I'll try to be kind to your mother in the paper tomorrow."

I stared at her, seeing her with my artist's eye as curiosity took control of her features making her eyes, ears, and mouth seem larger. "There is no scoop. My mother has always done what she thinks is right, and she thought it was right to be truthful with the voters of this district."

"But why now is the question. She has to realize her honesty is going to cost her a lot of votes. Maybe the election," the reporter said.

"My mother is the best candidate, and the voters will remember that when they cast their ballots."

"That's the way it's supposed to be, kid, but hardly anything is the way it's supposed to be and especially in politics," the woman said. "Actually I like your mother, but she'd have been smart to have waited a month to bare her soul to the people. By then they would have been her constituency and maybe a mite readier to forgive old transgressions. Voters are fickle." The woman looked at me. "So you're not going to give me anything I can use."

"I'm proud of..."

"Of my mother," the woman said the last few words for me. "I'll bet I've got that on tape fifty times, kid. For the sake of variety, you should come up with some new answers every once in a while."

I couldn't keep from smiling then, but it wasn't my political smile. "I guess I have been pretty boring."

"But you've never said anything that could possibly hurt your mother's chances. The perfect political offspring."

"I'm not sure that's true." My smile faded. If Mom lost the election, it would all be because of me, me and Nicky.

Martha Long's eyes sharpened on me as if she had caught my thought, but just at that moment Rick came up behind us and said, "Come on, Erin. We're waiting for you."

"It's been nice talking to you, Miss Long," I said.

"I'm the one who did all the talking," the woman said. "But what the heck, maybe I'll be kind to your mother anyway. Honesty needs a shot in the arm every once in a while, and if she finds the long-lost kid, it'd make a great human-interest piece. You'll let me know if she finds him, won't you, Erin?"

"I'm sure everybody will know."

"Just make sure I'm the first one, okay, kid?" She pushed a card with her telephone number on it out to me, then winked at Rick. "This one's a born politician. You never catch her off her practiced lines."

Rick watched her walk away before he said, "Are you going to call her when you find Nicky?"

I shoved the woman's card in my pocket. "We may never find him, and then Mom will have done all this for nothing."

"Not for nothing, Erin. For you."

"I feel so guilty. I know how much she wanted to win."

"She hasn't lost yet," Rick said. "My mother is already organizing the Concerned Citizens for a phone canvas to call every voter in the district."

"What about Evelyn Harris?"

"Mom says she took to her bed, but if I know Mrs. Harris, she'll not only be on the phone before the afternoon is out, she'll have Jason sending out computer messages as well." Rick grinned at me.

When I didn't smile back, he went on. "Don't look so worried, Erin. I mean we may have to go back to the smile if you're going to keep frowning so much.''

''I just wish I could be sure we were going to find him and that it isn't all some kind of dirty trick my imagination is playing on me.''

''You can be sure. You're going to find him.''

Rick was right. Nicky wasn't hard to find at all. The first adoptee search group Mom talked to pulled his name up right away on their computer. Nicholas Grant, age eighteen, medical emergency. His file was flagged for priority handling.

We flew south that afternoon. Nicky's adopted mother met us at the airport and drove us to the hospital to meet him.

Nicky had leukemia, she explained to Mom as she drove. The disease was in remission for the second time, but the doctors couldn't promise how long that would last. His only chance was a bone marrow transplant, if they could find a match. With siblings there was a one-in-four chance of a match.

''Of course, the odds go down with half sisters.'' She glanced over her shoulder to me in the back seat. ''The doctors warned us not to get our hopes up.''

''We'll match,'' I said quietly in answer to Mom's stricken look at me.

Nicky sat by the hospital window waiting for us. He was even slimmer than I'd drawn him in my sketches and his hair was very thin. The treatments, he explained, and started to put on a baseball cap.

"You don't have to put on that hat," I said. "I didn't mean to stare. It's just that you look so much like my sketches of you."

Our mothers had gone in search of coffee, and Nicky and I were alone.

"Did you bring them?" he asked. "Your sketches."

"Yes." I held out my sketchbook. "I thought I might want to draw on the plane ride down here, but I was too nervous."

He smiled. "Can I look at them?"

He turned through the pages slowly, stopping at the sketch of the two of us floating through the clouds and the rainbows.

"Do you remember that?" I asked him.

In answer he took a creased paper out of his pocket and handed it to me. Carefully I unfolded the picture I'd drawn for him so many years ago.

We stared at each other over the drawings for a moment before he said, "I want you to know, Rennie, that even if the transplant doesn't work out, I'm glad you came. I'm glad you're my sister."

I reached over and took his hand. After all these years it seemed funny to actually be touching him.

On the day of the election back home, the doctors drew out vials of my bone marrow and began giving it to Nicky. Since Mom was at the hospital with me, she had to make her acceptance speech by phone.

Later when I talked to Rick, he told me it was Martha Long's stories in the paper that had made the difference, and I was glad I'd saved her telephone number. She'd even come down and taken pictures of us at the hospital, but Nicky and I didn't tell her the whole truth.

Rick was the only person who knew the whole truth. He was waiting at the house when we got home from the airport. Mom went off with Dad to some kind of press conference, but they didn't make me go.

Instead Rick and I climbed up to the tower room where I moved slowly through the afternoon sunlight to the easel in the middle of the room. After a moment I said, "It'll be a while before they know if the transplant is going to work."

"It'll work," Rick said.

"How do you know?" I looked around at him.

"I'm psychic." Rick grinned. When I didn't smile, he added, "Come on, Erin. You've got to believe that so Nicky will make it."

I looked back at the canvas. "Do you mind if I paint for a while?"

Rick sat in the window and read while I mixed colors and began covering the blue. Once again I painted the shapes of my family—Mom's and Dad's, mine, Great-grandfather Winter's, my other grandparents' and finally Nicky's.

When I stepped back from the canvas, I had a good, strong feeling inside that Nicky was going to make it.

Rick came to stand behind me. He studied the shapes on the canvas. "I'm not sure what you've put there, but something about it makes me feel better." He put his arms around me, and I leaned back against him while I pointed out how the shapes represented my family.

At last he said, "Someday I'll have a family like that. Sisters, brothers, a past."

"You already have them, Rick." I turned to look up at him.

"I know," he said, his eyes still on the painting. "If only I can find them."

"You will," I said.

His eyes came away from the painting to meet mine. "I hope I have a sister just like you, Erin." Then just before he kissed me, he smiled and added, "But I'm glad it turned out that you weren't her."

After Rick went home, I sat in the window seat and mixed colors. I was too drained and tired to paint any more, but I wanted to stay in the tower room where I felt close to Nicky.

The colors I mixed were warm and bright, yet soft too. The colors that ran through my mind when Rick and I kissed. I looked at the canvases stacked against the walls and wondered if it would be possible to capture the colors of a kiss.

I laughed at the thought. How could I possibly think anything was impossible ever again? I had found Nicky.

I looked at the painting in the middle of the room. Later when I'd rested, I'd draw a sketch of the idea to send to Nicky. I'd promised to write to him every day until he was out of the hospital, but a drawing would be as good as a letter. Maybe better.

As I started down the stairs, I heard a whisper in the room behind me. I looked back, but it was only the wind against the windows or maybe even Great-grandfather Winters rattling his chains.

* * * * *

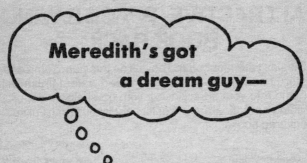

Meredith's got a dream guy—

in fact, she dreamed him up. But all her friends think he's real, and they can't wait to meet him. They're expecting Meredith to bring him to the school dance.

What's she going to do now?

Read **MY FUNNY VALENTINE** by Tessa Kay and find out.

Coming from Keepsake in . . . February, of course.